TOP HAND

**Center Point
Large Print**

**This Large Print Book carries the
Seal of Approval of N.A.V.H.**

TOP HAND

Wade Everett

CENTER POINT PUBLISHING
THORNDIKE, MAINE

This Center Point Large Print edition
is published in the year 2011 by arrangement with
Golden West Literary Agency.

The text of this Large Print edition is unabridged.
In other aspects, this book may vary
from the original edition.
Printed in the United States of America
on permanent paper.
Set in 16-point Times New Roman type.

ISBN: 978-1-61173-128-6

Library of Congress Cataloging-in-Publication Data

Everett, Wade.
Top hand / Wade Everett.
p. cm.
ISBN 978-1-61173-128-6 (lib. bdg. : alk. paper)
1. Large type books. I. Title.
PS3553.O5547T67 2011
813′.54—dc22

2011007617

1

ONE THING for sure, there were only two ways you could go when you met Charlie Hatch for the first time; you either took to him like a tick on a warm dog or you hated him on general principles. He was about twenty-four when I first met him, rather tall, and as thin as a creek willow. He had a shock of light, wavy hair and very mild blue eyes. His skin was lighter than most men who spend their life out in the weather and in the summer time he freckled badly.

I've never been sure whether I saw him first or whether he saw me; it's hard to tell because Charlie Hatch always saw more than he let on. I was sitting on the west bank of the Tongue, pouring water out of my boots when I saw a rider on a ridge, and he started down toward me. During five days of walking now I'd been aware that I was on someone's land because I knew beef work and I had seen branded stock.

Charlie Hatch came on and dismounted. He took out his tobacco and rolled a smoke, then handed it to me, all the time looking me over real careful but not making any point of it. He could tell I'd done cowboying, even though my boots were plumb walked out and my brush jacket was out at the elbows and my jeans were worn to a frazzle.

After he'd offered a match for my smoke, he

said, "I guess I don't have to tell you it's dangerous for a man to be afoot in this country. A critter will charge a man afoot."

There was something in his tone of voice that I liked; he talked out even to me, not down or hard like most white folks do. I said, "This tobacco's mighty good. It's been some time since I've had a pleasure like this."

"Lose your horse?"

"Mule," I told him. "Some forty miles back."

"That's a far piece to walk," he said, and turned to his saddle for his canteen. When he offered it to me I hesitated for I came from Texas where you don't drink from a white man's well, let alone his canteen. "Shit, it's all right," he said, and squatted down, making the batwings of his chaps flare out.

We smoked another cigaret and then he went to his saddlebag and brought back a cloth sack. He offered me a cold pancake wrapped around some strips of bacon and motioned for me to keep the canteen until I was done eating. "I'm Charlie Hatch," he said, and offered his hand.

"Buster Mills," I said.

"Texas? Thought so. Looking for work?"

I had a mouthful so I nodded.

He made a very broad sweep with his hand. "I'm foreman of this division. Three days ride in any direction. When you're through there we can ride double to Moon Creek. Pay's forty a month and found. Ten more for rough string ridin'. O. B. Hardison owns this spread, branding Broken T. Bullmoose Reilly is general foreman of the three divisions, a man who'll give you no trouble." He stood up. "The law after you?"

"No more," I said, and wondered if I should tell him.

I owned a saddle and the clothes on my back and Charlie Hatch mounted, then gave me a hand up behind him, and we turned north, working toward the ridges where the brush was less thick. We followed a game trail for some time. Then I saw some riders working a valley and branding calves; we cut down into it and made for the chuck wagon and horse corral.

We dismounted and Charlie Hatch gave me his catch rope and I picked out a horse, made my throw and saddled. Hatch was at the fire with a cup of coffee and when I was ready to leave, he shied the grounds away, tossed the cup in the wagon and stepped into the saddle.

At the head of the valley we came to a road and followed it for two hours and finally raised a cluster of low log buildings crouched against a backdrop of good timber. The main house was impressive enough, with at least six good rooms and as many stone fireplace chimneys.

The bunkhouse was built into a square with a center court and it was halfway between the house and the barn, with a large cookshack west of it. A corral large enough to hold three hundred head of horses fronted a large expanse of pasture.

We dismounted and tied up in front of the main house. "Come on in," Charlie Hatch said, and opened the door.

The beams were twelve by twelves, hand-hewn and at the end of the huge hall a stone fireplace took up all the wall. Hatch opened a side door and we stepped into his office, furnished with a roll-top desk and a big table covered with record books and papers and shipping invoices.

He took down a leather-covered book with the Broken T brand burned into it, and I noticed that the chairs and table and desk also bore that brand.

He wrote my name in the book and showed me where to sign, or to put my mark; I'm not sure what he expected. But I wrote my name neatly and he said nothing, just closed the book and put it back in the desk.

Then we went out and crossed the hall and he unlocked the door to another room. It was crammed with shelves of blankets and clothing and coiled rope and everything a ranch hand would need. Hatch said, "Miles City is some twenty miles away and we can't be runnin' into town all the time, so each division has a storeroom." He looked at me carefully, then started laying out clothes: underwear, socks, boots, gloves, two hickory shirts, a cotton shirt, brush jacket, slicker, two pairs of Frisco jeans, blankets, waterproof canvas, a heavy clasp knife, whetstone, four sacks of smoking tobacco, a plug of Star chewing tobacco, and a small sack of sugar hards. He grinned and said, "They're mighty pleasant on night guard, Buster. And I never knew a man who didn't have a sweet tooth." He wrote all these items down in a book and spun it around for me to sign. "Comes out of your pay." He pointed. "Price is right there, twenty-six dollars. Same as the brand paid." He watched me write my name. "You do that pretty good. Had some schoolin'?"

"Six grades," I said. "And I'm fond of reading."

He didn't let on one way or another what he thought of that, but he didn't seem to resent it, like most did.

I changed my clothes from the skin out and when I was through I went into the hall and found him in his office. He said, "Here's a note. Go back to the valley where the crew was workin' calves. Give this to Sad-eye Nolan; anyone will point him out to you."

"I do thank you, Mr. Hatch."

He grinned. "The name's Charlie and if I hear you call me mister again I'll kick your black ass."

I was surprised to find that I felt no anger at all, as I should have, but he said it easy, like an old friend talking and I laughed and went out to my horse.

That was how I began with Broken T in the

spring of 1887 and when that summer ended and the fall beef work was done and I found out that I was going to be kept on the winter, I wondered how come I had ever worked for anyone else.

Sad-eye Nolan was a runt; there wasn't any other way to describe him. Forty some, he had a reputation for being a pretty bad man when riled and he'd already spent five years in a Texas prison for armed robbery. He gave me a dirty job right off, riding bog, and because I was new to the country, he sent a cowboy named Hardpan with me.

For three weeks we combed the waterholes, freeing stock that were bogged down, stuck in the mud. The cold Montana winters weakened the stock and some of them would wade into the waterhole and be too weak to get out. Or else they were shoved in by the crowding.

Hardpan and I used our catch ropes, pitching a loop over the horns. The best way to free a steer is by a horn catch, pulling him straight out on his back. Now and then it's necessary to dismount and wade in and pull his legs out. Then you take hold of the tail and get him standing.

It makes exciting work because the danged critter will usually turn and charge the dismounted man.

So we rode bog and gathered weak stock and cows with early calves, and then we took a team and a slip scraper and spent a month cleaning out waterholes. All of it was tough work, but I had no complaints.

The food was good and there was plenty of it and I put on fifteen pounds without half trying and hammered it all down into good muscle.

Hardpan had no other name, or none that he could recollect. In years I'd judge him to be about fifty or maybe a bit older. He was medium built and he chewed tobacco all the time.

We got along because he wasn't a nosey man and all he knew was beef work, which was a pretty safe topic. There wasn't anything that went on that concerned the brand that he didn't know, and he knew a lot about other people's business.

His favorite was Charlie Hatch; you could tell that because he'd talk about Charlie at the drop of a hat. I heard all about Charlie's pranks. He was always playing them on someone, like the time he threw a bunch of firecrackers down the chimney of the cook shack, or when he put soap shavings into the Christmas mashed potatoes. Hardpan never got tired of laughing at this, because as he recollected it, there wasn't a bush that didn't shelter someone with his britches down.

And I learned about Jim Candless, who was foreman of the western division in Rosebud County. Jim had been courting a girl in Miles City and finally they set the day for the wedding. Unknown to Candless, Charlie Hatch began salting his coffee with saltpeter and on Candless' wedding night he couldn't do anything and the bride had cried and it nearly ruined the whole honeymoon.

Hardpan warned me that my turn would come and it wouldn't do any good to watch for it because Charlie Hatch was clever enough to get a man when he least expected it.

And I wondered if anyone had ever "gotten" Charlie Hatch.

Hardpan admitted that they had, last spring.

Bullmoose Reilly, the general foreman, started it off by spreading the word that he had a horse no one could ride and if any man had guts enough to stick on him for six seconds that man would get a month off with pay.

It was the kind of a thing Charlie Hatch couldn't resist and he accepted immediately. All the men came in to see it because they were in on how it was going to go. Bullmoose Reilly brought in a narrow-chested mustang with the wildest eyes ever seen on a horse and it took five good men just to get the saddle on him.

And while Charlie wasn't looking, a bunch of firecrackers were tied to the outlaw's tail.

Just before the blindfold was whipped off, the match was struck and everyone ran for cover. Charlie Hatch found himself perched on the biggest, noisiest cyclone to ever hit Wyoming. That horse turned belly up, landed spraddle-legged, did three turns on a ten cent piece, came unglued in five directions at one time, bit chunks out of Charlie's chaps, and for the six seconds Charlie hung onto the horn with both hands, between him and the saddle there was enough space to drive a young heifer.

The upshot of it was that Charlie was pitched badly, landing on the corral fence and breaking his right leg below the knee. Immediately everyone rushed to him, sorry the joke had gotten out of hand and they all thought Charlie had been done in good because he'd gone up pretty high before coming down so hard.

But Charlie was sitting in the dust and manure, nose bleeding, hat gone, shirt torn half off, laughing a blue streak. He'd stayed on the six seconds and now Bullmoose Reilly owed him one month off with full pay.

And I guess Bullmoose never did figure out who the joke was on because Charlie Hatch was made divisional roundup boss by the Cattle Association and he was gone for nearly two months.

It does take awhile for a man, any man, to understand the staggering dimensions of a brand such as Broken T. And I don't suppose the average rider ever got a good inkling of what the details of running such holdings were.

The O. B. Hardison headquarters was not on his ranch; it was located on a five-acre plot a few miles south of Miles City, and it was almost two years before I ever put foot inside it. And that was unusual because very few of the Broken T hands had ever been in the house.

However that's neither here nor there. Broken T constituted a large piece of land, including a good piece of Custer County, a thirty-five section nibble of Powder River County, and a middling chunk of Rosebud County.

Broken down in divisions, Andy Birch was the foreman in Powder River County and he carried a winter payroll of thirty men, and a summer payroll of over sixty.

In Rosebud County, Jim Candless was foreman, carrying fifty men in the winter and over a hundred in the summer.

Hardpan did admit that he knew Candless and Birch on sight, and one or two of the older hands, but generally he never got over into those counties except when on roundup crew, and they rarely came into his division, so the only way you could tell a Broken T man was by the brand on horse, saddle, chaps, and damned near everything he owned.

Charlie Hatch's division was not the largest, but somehow every man felt that it was more important than the others, which wasn't so but still it made for a good crew.

These were the knights of O. B. Hardison's round table, four men and the king on whose decision rested the social and economic prosperity of quite a few people and a few towns. And if that weren't impressive enough, a man could consider the empire of Canby Childress, to the east, branding Box O; he also sprawled over three counties, with headquarters at Locate on the Powder River.

To the north lay the Boxley land, branding Leaning S, and a lot of smaller shotgun outfits running on only four or five sections.

It made a man almost feel sorry for them to think of it.

Mid-summer came and we were pulled off water hole cleaning and put to haying and it was then that I learned about the farmers. According to Hardpan, the farmers had been invited to settle there, sold the land at rock bottom prices, and guaranteed a market for their produce. All without one whit of trouble from the cattlemen.

This was good for O. B. Hardison because it guaranteed his winter hay and put fresh produce on the mess table, which included eggs and ham, a rarity on the range. And it gave the farmers security and a profit, which is really the thing that keeps a man going anyway.

While Hardpan and I were riding bog and cleaning water holes and haying, and some of the crew were branding calves and castrating and dehorning, the spring roundup was underway, a combined effort of four hundred men that ranged over eight counties.

Charlie Hatch was again division roundup

foreman and I didn't see him all summer, or early fall either because a big outfit like Broken T shipped about three times a year, and when that was done the fall roundup began.

That was real beef work with calf branding again and the bulls to be gathered so they could be fed during the winter. Hardpan and I brush popped for about two weeks; then Charlie Hatch rode up and put us on calf weaning so their mothers could have a better chance with the coming winter.

And winter came quick in this high country. Even in September the air turned nippy when the sun went down and a man could see his breath when he rolled out in the morning. A man worked from dawn to dark because there was always a lot to be done and never enough time to do it, but finally it was finished and we quit the range for a spell.

We made our headquarters at Moon Creek and I expected a little trouble because all the old hands already had their bunks picked out and I'd either have to wait until they'd settled in or run into a fist fight because I'd thrown my gear on one that was taken.

The Dingo Kid solved this for me when he said, "Buster, you take this one."

There wouldn't be any argument because none of the hands argued with The Dingo Kid. He was young, in his early twenties, and from Australia, and he always wore a funny, hard-crowned hat with a narrow brim in the front; it was some kind of a military hat, a sailor's dress hat, or a soldier's; I didn't know which. And he talked somewhat like an Englishman, with a peculiar, broad "a" sound.

Hardtack had immediately informed me of The Dingo Kid's reputation as a thoroughly dangerous man and I halfway expected trouble from him, because a long time before I had learned that while red will set a bull off, black will do for a man.

But there had been no trouble at all; I did my work well and never hung back and somehow The Dingo Kid became one of my friends.

I met Bullmoose Reilly that afternoon, when paycall was sounded on the headquarters porch and we lined up for it, the older hands first, then the rough string riders, the newer hands, and the horse wranglers; there was a definite caste system in the cattle business.

Reilly was certainly well named; he was of a size that could easily hunt bear with a willow switch. He was six foot four in his stocking feet and he had shoulders at least an ax handle wide. His face was knobby and the veins on his cheekbones were near the surface of the skin, little red streaks darting off in all directions.

He called out our names and we stepped forward and Charlie Hatch paid out the money, in hard coin because paper money still made some men suspicious. It was here that Hatch would pick his winter crew and I'm not sure how he did it because some of the men who had been on Broken T for six summers were let go.

It wasn't a thing to make a hand sore; cowboying in the high country is pretty much a spring to fall job. Hatch would pay a man and ask him if he wanted to work out the winter; if a man wanted to go south where the sun shone he turned it down, but most stayed on although winter work was hard, lonely, and pretty dangerous.

Finally the line melted away and the hands were mounting up, getting ready to go into Miles City and lap the saloons dry; it was my turn to be paid and Charlie Hatch said, "Bullmoose, this is Buster Mills. He's worked out mighty fine for us."

Reilly smothered my hand in his and I'm not a small man. "It's a good brand, Buster. We like good men."

Hatch counted out my pay. "Do you want to stay on the winter, Buster?"

I was genuinely surprised. "Sure do, Mis—" I cut it off quickly and grinned, for Charlie Hatch had started to get up. "Charlie?"

He grinned and pulled the brim of my hat down over my eyes. Before I could step out of line and let the next man up, Hatch said, "I've got a hundred and fifty head of calves to drive up to the Potter Place in Garfield County. I asked The Dingo Kid to pick a crew for me. He asked for Dandy McGee, Sad-eye Nolan, and you. All right?"

"Sure thing, all right."

"Don't run off to town then. We'll leave in the morning."

I pocketed my pay, and it felt good, that money, good because I'd worked my hands hard-callused for it and I wasn't going to go spending it on whiskey and whores either.

The Dingo Kid and Dandy McGee were in the bunkhouse when I stepped inside; most of the others had put on their town clothes and left for town to whoop it up. The Dingo Kid was loading a pearl-handled .44 and he slipped it into a spring shoulder holster, then shrugged on his sheepskin vest.

"You own a gun, Buster?" he asked.

I shook my head. He rummaged in his bag and handed me a short-barreled Merwin-Hulbert .44, saying, "Put that in your chap pocket, Buster, but don't let on like you got it."

"What do I need a gun for?"

He winked. "Garfield County's a far piece from here, Buster, and you never can tell what you'll run into."

I wasn't going to push it any further or argue; a man learns a lot more when he keeps his mouth shut. Dandy McGee had a revolver and shell belt laid out; he was oiling the mechanism carefully, then he slipped it into the holster, rolled the belt around it and put it away.

I bring all this up because until now I'd never seen a side arm displayed on the Broken T and figured there was some kind of a rule against it; the big outfits had rules like that to keep trouble down. Most everyone carried a rifle because there were bear and wolves about and all summer I'd carried a .40-82 Winchester that belonged to the brand and thought nothing of it, but I hadn't seen one pistol anywhere.

Charlie Hatch came in later that afternoon. The Dingo Kid was sleeping and Dandy McGee was over at the cook shack, seeing what he could talk the cook into feeding him; the man ate as though he fed a tapeworm.

I was on my bunk, reading a month old Billings paper.

Charlie Hatch came up and laid a holstered pistol on the bunk. Then The Dingo Kid said, "I already gave him one."

"Thought you were asleep," Charlie said.

"You know I sleep light, Charlie."

He swung his feet to the floor and sat up. Charlie Hatch glanced at him, then said, "Tell you how it is, Buster. Potter has a pretty nice spread south of Little Dry Creek, and he's been trying to build up his herd. Now Simon Boxley of Leaning S, who is Potter's neighbor, thinks that's a very bad idea, and he doesn't like to see Broken T sell stock to Potter. Especially Hereford heifers. Beginnin' to understand?"

"Some now." I said. "If there's trouble, I don't mind. I was born to it."

"He ain't ever owned a gun," The Dingo Kid said dryly.

"That so?" Hatch asked.

It seemed important, so I said, "That's so, but I can make real threatenin' motions with one, if I have to."

Hatch laughed and it seemed to satisfy The Dingo Kid. "You'll do to ride with, Buster," he said, and stretched out on his bunk again. Then he said, "How old are you, Buster?"

"When I'm happy or when I'm sad?" I asked.

"How about in between?"

"Thirty-one," I told him. "But don't get me nothing for my birthday."

He thought that was funny and Charlie Hatch picked up the gun he had brought me. "There isn't much of a crew here tonight, but Raunchy will fix up a good meal. Buster, you see him in the morning with two pack horses. He'll have our grub ready."

I nodded, then touched his arm. "Charlie, where could I get some paper and an envelope? I want to send a letter and some money."

"I'll give you paper and an envelope," he said. "But the money you'll have to send by telegram. You tell me how much you want to send and I'll see that it goes out." He looked at me, read my expression, then said, "That's no good, huh?"

"It wouldn't do for people to know this party got some money," I said.

"Why don't you wrap the money in paper and put it in a wooden cartridge box," Charlie Hatch said. "You want to do that? It wouldn't rattle or nothing." He took my arm and brought me down off the bunk. "Come on to the house and we'll fix you right up."

I went with him and he gave me the box and the wrapping paper and some old newspapers to stuff around the money, but I could see that it wasn't going to work and that I couldn't solve it by myself.

"Charlie, I want to send a hundred dollars, but if this person ever showed a twenty dollar gold piece there'd be big trouble." He looked at me and waited a moment to see if I was going to tell him any more.

I wasn't.

"How would dollars do? Take a little bigger box."

He took my money and went into his office and the safe and brought it back in silver. When I took it, I said, "Charlie, I'd like to tell you—"

He shook his head. "A man's business is his own. I don't pump anybody. When you finish, leave it on my desk. Bullmoose will have it mailed tomorrow."

2

DRIVING A herd sixty miles didn't seem like much to me; I'd been north from Texas, clean to Kansas twice. The herd had been gathered and was being held in a pasture southwest of Moon Creek; we picked it up there and started north. I rode drag while the others rode flankers and if the leaders started to bunch quit or swing, why Charlie or The Dingo Kid would just cut through and swing them back.

It was an easy drive although the country was mountainous. That night we'd made ten miles and I could see that Charlie wasn't going to push the stock gaunt. At the end of the second day we crossed the Yellowstone west of Miles City and then on north and day by day the land began to change, flattening out a little, but never less than deep rolling hills with timber furry on the flanks and brush in the clearings.

The great mountains lay far to the west, but on a clear day you could see them, reaching up into the clouds like a rocky hand thrust into cotton.

You could tell by the land, the grass, and the trees that this part of the country got hot in the summer because it had a parched look, as though it had suffered through a long, dry spell. Working the summer had taught me something about the weather; that it could roast you at midday, take a twenty degree drop in temperature, then let go a cloudburst come evening that would set every dry wash to roaring and spilling its banks.

We followed Sunday Creek for three days, then cut due north again, into open land. The timber was thin and in many places there wasn't any at all except some larch and scrub pine; the country seemed to be either timbered or brushy and there were no bare plains at all, which seemed odd to a Texas man.

On the afternoon of the seventh day we crossed into Teepee land and we camped at the foot of a long valley with a good creek splitting it down the middle. Time on the trail had demonstrated that Sad-eye Nolan burned food only rarely, so Charlie Hatch had him build up a humdinger of a fire and we drew lots for night guard.

It wasn't hard to see how Sad-eye got his name, for some injury or muscle defect allowed his right eyebrow to sag and it seemed that he was squinting all the time. He cooked up a fine meal, pan biscuits, sonofabitch stew, and corned tomatoes.

And he made plenty of it.

Come nightfall, a knot of riders came toward us from the north; they rode right through the herd and flung off. One of them led their horses to the picket line and the rest came on to the fire.

Ardy Potter was an elderly man, quite tall, and he had a long, hooked nose and a chin that came right out to a point. His mustache had never known a razor and I'm sure it draped at least six or seven inches on each side of his mouth and the wind stirred it like some gossamer cloth.

A wave of Potter's hand sent his men back into the saddle and they took charge of the herd. He and Charlie Hatch squatted by the fire and rolled cigarets and talked.

"Tomorrow we'll ride into Crow Rock and settle up," Potter said. "The money's in the express office safe, ten thousand five hundred. That's right, ain't it?"

"You want a tally?"

"Hell no! Hardison wouldn't cheat me or anyone else." He chuckled. "A long time I've wanted some purebred heifers and a couple of young bulls. And I've got a bobwire fence up between me and Boxley to keep what I've paid for."

It was a word to make me tune in my ears, bobwire. I'd lived through wars over that stuff and to me it meant trouble, like saying gun and thinking shoot.

Dandy McGee and The Dingo Kid came in and moved up to the fire.

Potter said, "You fellas held up any stages lately?"

"We don't do things like that anymore," McGee said and winked at The Dingo Kid.

"Not in Montana anyway," Dingo put in.

Then Potter looked at me, not through me or down to me; he looked at me and measured me like he would any man and I knew right off that he wasn't a southern gentleman. "You new to Broken T?"

"Signed on in the spring," I said.

He pursed his lips. "Winter work already? You must have proved up in a hurry."

Sad-eye Nolan said, "He keeps his nose out of people's business, his hands busy, and his ass in the saddle." He winked at me. "You stay on five years and old man Hardison puts a big Broken T brand on the left cheek of your ass. Ain't that right, Charlie?"

"Why ask me?" Hatch said. "Take down your pants and show him."

"Hell with that," Sad-eye said and got the tin plates. We lined up and ladled the stew, then Potter called his men in two at a time to eat.

This is always a good time for range men. The talk is good and the laughter is easy and the boss is just a man like you are and the work doesn't seem so hard then, or the loneliness so acute.

Charlie Hatch played the mouth organ and he played quite well and normally I'd have kept my mouth shut, but the music got to me, and the talk, and I up and admitted that I played the banjo.

"By God now," Sad-eye said, "wouldn't that be the ticket? No offense, Charlie, but that mouth organ playin' does get wearin' after a year or two." He looked at me. "You play jigs and reels, Buster?"

"Play about anything you want, Sad-eye."

The Dingo Kid said, "Why don't we get Buster a banjo?" He dug into his pocket for two dollars and tossed them in his coffee cup before passing it around. "Come on now, shell out and we'll turn Crow Rock upside down and see if we can't get Buster a banjo." He got up and made sure that everyone divvied up, then put the money in his pocket, saying, "Since I've had professional experience taking charge of other people's money, I'll just hold onto this. I hear no objections?"

There were none and the matter was settled.

We rolled in a few minutes later and I lay awake, my feelings pulled in two directions by this. It touched me to think that they'd chip in to buy me a banjo; it was a warm, generous thing to do. Yet I couldn't help thinking that a banjo had nearly done me in and set my feet to moving as far out of Texas as I could get.

Come morning we got up at dawn, had breakfast, then mounted up and rode into Crow Rock with Ardy Potter. It was some hour and a half ride and the town wasn't much. But this was lonely country with places few and far between, so Crow Rock's single, rutted street looked pretty good.

Everything was log construction for wood was easy to get, especially lodgepine. There were a few back alleys and some houses built on the rise of a hill behind the main street, but the town was that one street with the stores and saloon and hotel bracketing it.

We tied up in front of Frizby's store and express office and while Charlie Hatch and Ardy Potter went inside to settle money matters, we walked a way down and went into the saloon. It was a room nearly forty foot square and the bar ran along the west wall, huge planks spiked to four saw horses. There were some tables and four men sat around one, shoulders hunched in their buffalo coats.

By preference I'd have just as soon stayed in the store, but it was The Dingo Kid's invitation and I didn't want to offend him, or anyone else. When we sidled up to the bar, the owner looked at us, but really looked at me, and when he spoke, it was to Dandy McGee and the others, not me.

"What'll ya have?"

"Let's try the whiskey," Sad-eye said, "and spill a little. If it don't discolor the wood, we'll drink it."

The bartender seemed a bit offended and he slid three glasses out and The Dingo Kid said, "One more, friend."

"Look," the bartender protested, "I didn't say nothin' when you came in, but I'm from Texas and—"

"You ain't in Texas now," Sad-eye reminded

28

him, and snapped his fingers. The bartender looked as though he was going to object, but he decided against it and produced another glass. He poured and The Dingo Kid offered a toast. "Here's to long summers and wild women." Then he turned around suddenly and looked at the four men sitting at the table. "You been waiting for Broken T to come to town, Boxley?"

The old man had his back to us and he turned slowly and looked at all of us standing there. "I'll wait for Charlie Hatch," he said and turned back.

"Sure, you do that," Dingo said, and we had our drink. He wiggled his head and the bartender came up. "Say, you know if there's a banjo anywhere in town?"

"Banjo?"

"That's a musical instrument," Dingo said.

"I know what it is. Just tryin' to think. Say, try at the end of the street at the stable. Seems to me that last year he held a saddle and banjo for a fella who never came back to square his bill."

"Thanks," The Dingo Kid said. "You wait here; I'll be right back." He went out and we stood there, holding up the bar and wondering what was keeping Charlie Hatch.

Old man Boxley spoke in a loud voice. "How 'bout some more coffee here? The service is rotten, High-pockets."

"Esther!" He yelled and a young girl came from the back room. She was raw-boned and a long

29

way from being pretty because her nose was too big and her eyes were a little too close together and her hair was without luster. She also seemed a bit frightened and when she poured another round of coffee for the Boxleys she had to use both hands, and still she trembled.

The front door opened and Charlie Hatch came in, a leather sack in his hand. He nodded to us and we went over to a table and sat down. Esther was through pouring coffee but she stood there and looked at Charlie Hatch, who said, "We could use something to eat, Esther."

"Oh, yes," she said and dashed into the kitchen. Then she came back and Charlie Hatch grinned at her and she blushed and batted her eyes. He took her hand, which surprised me, and then he brushed his lips lightly against the back of it.

"My little mountain blossom, you get prettier every time I see you, which ain't often enough."

"Oh, Charlie," she said, and giggled and looked at the floor.

He smiled again. "You just bring us what you've got, Esther. Don't fuss special for us. All right?"

She managed to nod and turned away, giggling. Sad-eye Nolan said, "How can you do it, Charlie? Will you tell me that?"

"What does it cost to be nice?"

"I give up," Nolan said and rolled a cigaret.

Charlie Hatch looked around the room, at the Boxleys, and at us, then he said, "Buster, I want to ask you somethin'. You know, I ain't ever once heard you cuss."

"Well, Charlie, I don't hold much to it," I said.

Dandy McGee's attention sharpened. "By golly, that's right. I ain't ever heard you cuss either, Buster. You, Sad-eye?"

"Never did." He looked at me. "How come, Buster?"

"Truth is," I said, "I done some studying for the ministry. It's just that I don't hold with it. Don't bother me none to hear another man cuss, but I just get along without it."

Sad-eye Nolan seemed very impressed. "By golly, ain't that somethin' though? A preacher. Knew there was somethin' special about you, Buster. You're a good man with a catch rope, but I seen right away that you was good inside. No meanness in you at all."

Esther came with the food, a huge dish of stew and a stack of plates; she made three more trips, bringing stewed tomatoes and peas and a big dish of mashed potatoes and two peach pies.

On her last trip she brought a two gallon coffee pot and cups, then she looked at Hatch and said, "Is this all right, Charlie?"

"Delicious," he said and took her hands and kissed her fingers. "Did your little hands do this? Tell me?"

"Oh, Charlie!" She went into a fit of giggles and rushed to the kitchen again.

Sad-eye Nolan shook his head. "You sure take the cake, Charlie."

"She sure is homely though," Dandy McGee said.

They were joking, in a way that hurt a little, then I looked at Charlie Hatch, looked at his eyes and saw that they were serious. "She's a nice girl. Don't drink, cuss, or chew. If I had a sister I'd want her to be like Esther. Trouble with you fellas, you never look at her eyes. They're blue like a teal's wing and they got warmth in 'em like a summer sky. Ain't no lies in them eyes, I can tell you. No little heart there, boys. You fellas just don't see, that's all."

There was a moment of silence around the table, and I guess Charlie Hatch realized that he'd showed a bit more of himself than he'd intended and he laughed kind of embarrassed like and said, "Let's eat, huh?"

We heard The Dingo Kid coming down the street, heard the unskilled twanging of a banjo, then he came in, making a lot of noise on it and came over to our table.

He handed me the banjo; it was a good instrument, a five string tenor such as I had never been able to afford, with pearl inlays on the neck between the frets. Dingo sat down and filled his plate and Charlie Hatch said, "Give us a tune, Buster."

"Soon as I get it in tune," I said and made

adjustments. Finally I had it and wondered what I should play, something soft and slow to remind me of home and what I no longer had, or a spirited tune to bring out the smile in a man and make him tap his foot.

That was the kind all right and I began some real banjo plucking, a song called *Banjo Rag*. It was my feeling that they'd never heard banjo playing like that, but they had no way of knowing that I'd made my way with five strings and nimble fingers. A man like me didn't have much choice; you picked cotton or plowed someone else's bottom land or you made music for the white folks' pleasure. It helped to make you forget who you were and what you were and it paid good money, better by ten times than what you could make otherwise.

Esther had come in out of the kitchen and the bartender was smiling and some people out on the street heard it and came in to listen. I must have played five or six tunes, then old man Boxley scraped back his chair and came over and put his hand on my shoulder.

It was an enemy hand; you can tell, by the pressure of the fingers. He said, "Play *Nigger in the Woodpile*."

I didn't know that song and I didn't think there was a song like that, but I didn't know what to say.

Charlie Hatch bunched his muscles to rise, but Dandy McGee said, "Let me," and he hauled off and hit old man Boxley. Dandy was not a big man; I'd put him in the runt size, but somewhere he gathered his strength and the blow he fetched to Boxley would have felled a heifer.

The old man went back a good ten feet, slammed into the wall, bounced off, spun half around and crashed into the sawdust flat on his back and he wasn't about to stir a muscle.

I heard two pieces of leather snap together and when I looked at The Dingo Kid he had that pretty, pearl-handled .44 in his hand and was pointing it at the three Boxleys. They were frozen around the table, statues caught there. One had his hand on his pistol and the other was half up, the third had his mouth open and was staring.

The Dingo Kid said, "Now if I have to blow a couple of holes in you gentlemen, you'll bleed all over the sawdust. You didn't hurt your knuckles there, did you, Dandy?"

"Naw!" He looked at the old man. "Sure does look peaceful, don't he? Sleepin' like a baby, ain't he? To look at him you'd never think he was a mean old sonofabitch who got his start rustlin' cattle, would you?"

Sad-eye Nolan said, "That's pretty harsh, Dandy. You've sinned yourself, you know."

"That's true," McGee said and looked thoughtfully at the old man, who groaned and rolled his head slightly from side to side. "I'm sorry I called you a sonofabitch."

"Oh, that's much better," Sad-eye Nolan said. "Dingo, why don't you let a couple of them fine young boys come and get their old pap?"

"That sound all right to you, Charlie?" Dingo asked.

Hatch shrugged. "Guess so. You always were a generous cuss, Dingo." He got up and motioned for two of the Boxley boys to give him a hand and they lifted the old man to his feet. His lips were badly mashed and I suspected that he'd either chipped or lost a couple of teeth because he kept a hand clapped to his mouth.

They took him out, supporting him between them, and Charlie Hatch went as far as the door to see that they got started in the right direction. Ardy Potter came in just as the three Boxleys went out and he said, "Don't take them long to find trouble, does it?"

"Come on over," Charlie said. "We're havin' a little banjo music." He got a chair for Potter, then thought of something and went over to the youngest Boxley boy, reached inside his coat and withdrew his pistol. He broke it open and scattered the shells, then tossed it into the far corner. "Get out of here," Charlie said, "and try and behave yourself."

The boy left and Charlie sat down and took out his harmonica. "This thing's in G, Buster. You play in that key?"

"Play in any key you want, Charlie."

"Try this one," he said and began to play the *Battle Hymn of the Republic.*

Esther came to clear off the table and Charlie Hatch made her sit down and he put his arm around her and kissed her on the cheek and he wasn't getting smart with her, and darned if he didn't coax her to sing.

When he started that I had a few moments of doubt, but I said nothing; it's a habit that's kept me out of a lot of trouble. He was a hard man to resist and she really didn't have a chance.

Very timidly she said, "I only know one song."

"You just sing it," Charlie Hatch said softly, "and we'll find our way."

I would say that thirty men crowded into the place; they stood there in their heavy coats and solemn expressions; some chewed tobacco yet I didn't hear anyone spit.

She looked at Charlie Hatch and smiled and by golly she had the eyes all right; there was a life-light there that seemed to make everything a little brighter. And she looked at me and made me her slave, just like that.

Then she began to sing in a sweet, vibrato voice, softly, clearly, like distant bells pealing on a cold day: "My darling, I am dreaming, of the days gone by . . ."

I put the chords behind her, softly, gently on the strings and Charlie Hatch cupped his hands around his mouthorgan, smothering it so that his playing was only a muted background to her wonderful, sweet voice. To say that she was a great singer would be wrong; she sang beautifully because she thought beauty and believed beauty and no ugliness had ever touched her.

". . . when you and I were sweethearts, as in days gone by . . ."

I heard a man sniff and start to blow his nose, and someone must have nudged him for there was instant silence, and she sang on, in her own world, only she was letting us see it and she was taking us there and it was the best world I had ever known.

I looked at The Dingo Kid and his eyes were glistening as though he had been chousing a critter and running full tilt through brush and had been whipped across the face. And Dandy McGee was making snuffing sounds with his nose, twitching it like a rabbit scenting fresh clover.

Sad-eye Nolan looked at his hands and thought of mother and home and God knows what was in his past for they were all men with blots on their conscience, full of danger and loneliness and this girl with the crystal eyes and pure voice was wiping it all out as though she were some frocked priest in a darkened confessional. When I looked at Charlie Hatch I found him watching her, for of all of us, he had seen for himself what she now revealed to us and I wondered how he had done it. I wondered what sign had she made to him and not to us, and I decided that there had been none at all. He was just the kind of a man who saw things.

When she finished her song she sat there and looked at each of us as though she were not at all sure how she had done and wanted us to tell her. The men standing in the room shifted their feet and then someone applauded and they all took it up and Esther clasped her hands together and smiled, incredibly happy, as though she had been given the most wonderful gift.

Dandy McGee sniffed and said, "Esther, I guess you're the nicest girl I've ever known." Then he scraped back his chair and said, "I'm goin' to get me a drink," and he pushed through the crowd to the bar.

Esther looked a little alarmed, as though she had somehow caused him to do this, and Charlie Hatch patted her hand and said, "Dandy, he's kind of a sentimental cuss only he don't like to show it." Then he laughed. "That Buster plays some banjo, don't he?"

"Oh, yes," she said. "I hope my singin' didn't bother you none, because I don't know one note from another." Then she got up and brushed at her dress. "My, I shouldn't be sittin' here, all these people in here. I'll lose my job."

She was gone before Charlie could stop her, but I don't think he intended to. He hunched in his chair and took out his tobacco and rolled a cigaret. With it dangling from between his lips he hammered the spit out of his mouthorgan by tapping it against his palm. "Guess that's enough music for tonight," he said, and glanced at us.

Dandy McGee came back with bottle and glasses; he poured but we just let it set there. Then he said, "Charlie, is your ma alive?"

Hatch shook his head. "Fever took her when I was twelve. Two sisters too."

"Too bad," Dandy McGee said. Then he looked at me. "You got a family, Buster?"

A man doesn't lie when he's asked like that, feeling the way we were all feeling. I said, "Yes, a wife and two little girls."

"Well, I'll be damned," The Dingo Kid said. "I figured you for a family man, Buster. You got that look about you."

"What kind of look's that?" I asked.

"Like you was a man who cared about someone beside himself."

Charlie Hatch picked up his drink and held it and we did the same. "Here's to bitter tears."

"That's like toastin' a dose of clap," Sad-eye Nolan said, but tossed down his drink. When he banged down his glass he said, "What are we goin' to do? Stay here in town and wait for Boxley to come back with half his crew, or light out?"

"We didn't come here to fight," Hatch said. "Can we stay the night at your place, Ardy?"

"Sure," Potter said. "Leave when you've a mind to."

"Now's as good as any," Charlie Hatch said, and we got up and went outside to our horses.

As we rode out I took a look back. It was a different town now, and I liked this one better.

3

THE POTTER ranch buildings were located just south of Little Dry Creek, low, log buildings with mud chinking, but they were a welcome sight for it was late when we got there. I took charge of the horses, fed them and turned them into the corral with Potter's stock, then we found a place for ourselves in the bunkhouse.

The cook, beating on an old wagon rim, woke us and we went outside and washed in a chilled water tub. The air was nippy and it wouldn't be long before a man woke up to frost in the morning and ice on the horse trough.

Potter had a family, a wife, and three children, all grown. The two boys ate with the hands and lived in the bunkhouse, but the girl stayed in the main house. I never did see her, which was all right with me.

We had a breakfast of steak, potatoes, pan biscuits, and hot pie, and drank up all the coffee before Charlie Hatch told us to catch up our horses. We were leaving.

The cook gave Dandy McGee a huge sack of grub, enough to last us two days, and we all figured to make Miles City or the ranch at Moon Creek by then. Potter shook hands all around as we were getting ready to mount up, and he said to me, "Buster, I want to hear more of that banjo."

"If I get this way again," I said, and got into the saddle because Charlie and the others were mounted and already turning out of the yard. We rode directly south to the old road and followed it to a wide spot called Rock Springs; it was a store, a saddle shop, a saloon, and a stage depot. Charlie pulled us all up in front of the saloon and said, "Wait here." He dismounted and carried his saddlebags across to the stage depot and went inside. A few minutes later he came back, folding a piece of paper and putting it in his pocket. I noticed that the saddlebags were flatter and lighter now, and I understood that he'd entrusted the money with the stage line.

He mounted and backed his horse, saying, "Dingo, you and the others stay on the road." He reached back into his saddlebag and brought out a box of .44-40 cartridges, broke it open and dumped the contents into his mackinaw pocket. "I'll see you down the line, huh?" Then he grinned and rode out of town.

The Dingo Kid said, "It may turn out to be a lively day after all."

We left Rock Springs and stayed on the stage road as it dipped and rose and wiggled along the easiest southern route and I kept looking around at the timbered high reaches on both sides. Finally Sad-eye Nolan said, "You'll get a stiff neck doin' that, Buster."

It was a nice way of telling me to quit it, so I put my attention on the road ahead, letting the cresting of every rise be its own little surprise.

The Dingo Kid wasn't hurrying, but he wasn't poking along either, and about eight miles out of town we followed the road through a cutbank, then broke around a sharp corner and found a dozen mounted men sitting their horses.

I recognized old man Boxley and his sons and the others all rode Leaning S horses. We hauled up and waited and Boxley detached himself and rode forward a pace, looking from one to the other.

He said, "Where's Charlie Hatch?"

Sad-eye Nolan said, "He's drunk. We left him in Rock Springs."

"You're a liar," the old man said flatly.

Sad-eye shrugged. "It's always been my failing, I guess. You really shouldn't ask me anything then."

"You!" he said, looking at me.

"Who? Me?"

"Yes, you. Where's Hatch?"

I gave it to him the way he liked to hear it. "Not wit us, boss."

Boxley took a grip on his temper. "Damn it, you've bought more trouble than you can handle."

He pointed to Dandy McGee. "Get down off that horse or get dragged off."

From somewhere along the brushy ridge, Charlie Hatch called down. "You fellas go ahead and ride on. Mr. Boxley's through."

The old man turned his head and looked up and then Hatch's .44 Winchester coughed and Boxley's hat was plucked off and sailed alongside the road.

"You want to go ahead and think that was a near miss," Charlie Hatch invited, "then you go right ahead, Mr. Boxley."

"If we don't get on," the Dingo Kid said, "we ain't goin' to get home for tea and you know how angry that makes papa."

"You're so-o-o right," Sad-eye agreed. "Goodbye, gents. And do have fun with our friend up there in the brush. He's kind of shy, but if you let him shoot one or two of you, he'd get over it." He grinned and moved around the riders clogging the road and we followed him and as we passed on I noticed that Boxley's fallen hat had been badly trampled.

We went on, not wasting time, and that night we made night camp pretty high and stood guard while Dandy McGee rustled the grub. Then Charlie Hatch rode in and stepped out of the saddle.

"You been trailing us?" Sad-eye asked.

"Kind of," Hatch admitted, and toasted his

hands over the fire. "They're unpredictable bastards and it don't pay to chance anything. But they turned back right after you left."

We had coffee and ate some of the food Potter had given us, then rolled into our blankets. Charlie Hatch took the first guard and it was almost midnight when he woke me. The night was clear and cold and I'd never seen so many stars.

I did a two hour turn, then woke The Dingo Kid and went back to my blankets. Charlie Hatch was awake and smoking a cigaret. He said, "Every time I get a chance to shoot that old man I ain't got the heart to do it, Buster. It's beginnin' to worry me some."

"You ain't a shootin' man, Charlie. That's all there is to it."

I got out my tobacco to give me something to do; I could see that he wanted company. The others were sleeping soundly and The Dingo Kid was out of earshot, but we kept our voices low.

"You'll hear things about the Boxleys, Buster. In years past they've put rope around a few men's necks."

"Hanging?"

He bobbed his head. "Simon Boxley called 'em rustlers. Who knows what they were? Hangin's pretty permanent. You make a mistake and you can't undo it."

"The sheriff didn't do anything?"

"Well, there wasn't much he could do. We've

got one sheriff and he's in Miles City. Prairie County don't have a sheriff at all." He looked at me, and I expected him to say something, or ask me something, but he didn't. He snubbed out his smoke. "Better get some sleep."

Miles City, when we got to it, was what I called a real town. The streets were wide and the main street was four and a half blocks long, flanked solidly by stores. The hotel was a huge lodge, two stories, with a balcony running along the front, and on the slopes north of town there were at least six square blocks of residences. I could see the spire of the church and the school further on, and the courthouse occupied a whole block by itself.

When we rode in, Charlie Hatch pulled in at the hotel and dismounted. "You're free until tomorrow morning at Moon Creek," he said. "Stay out of trouble."

"Trouble," The Dingo Kid said. "What's that?" He grinned at Charlie Hatch, who went on into the hotel. The Dingo Kid looked around, letting his eyes move slowly up and down the street. "It's too early to get drunk."

"Not too early to get started on it," Dandy McGee said.

"Good point there. How about it, Sad-eye?"

Nolan shook his head. "I may hunt you up later."

"By golly, he's goin' courtin'," McGee said. "The widow Mersey." He laughed and slapped

The Dingo Kid on the arm. Then he pulled the brim of his hat down over both ears, puckered his face, and spoke in a piping falsetto. "Oh, my dear Mr. Nolan, this is such a surprise. And me in my skivvies too! Won't you come in, you dear, sweet boy. But please clean the cowshit off your boots because I just beat my parlor rug."

"Aw, cut it out," Sad-eye said, and I could see that it bothered him.

"Why don't the three of us take a sample at the saloon?" I said.

"Sure, Buster. Let Sad-eye go and break his heart." He winked at us and we turned our horses and rode across the street and down a way, then tied up in front of what seemed to be the biggest of the three saloons. We dismounted and crossed the boardwalk to the porch, but there The Dingo Kid stopped us with a raised hand. "Hold on. There goes Sad-eye toward Grady's barbershop. He'll soak in the tub and get shaved and shampooed and he'll come out of there smellin' like an El Paso whore. Come on."

I was not at all sure what he had in mind, but I knew it would be funny and very sad at the same time. Something told me to stay out of it, but I couldn't and I didn't want to.

We went back across the street to the drug store. The Dingo Kid bought some cigars and passed them around and he bought a jar of saddle soap, then he took the druggist by the sleeve and spoke confidentially. "What you got that'll itch like hell?"

The druggist reared back a little. "What's on your mind, Dingo?"

"A little joke. You ain't got a thing against a joke, have you?"

"On who?" the druggist asked.

The Dingo Kid wore his most winning manner, "Why, I thought it would be fun to slip a little itch powder in Sad-eye Nolan's longjohns." He winked. "He'll be over to the widow Mersey's tonight and—"

The druggist chuckled. "Hehehehehehe!" He looked at each of us. "Don't have any itching powder, Dingo, but cut up hair'll work like nothing you ever saw. Especially if a man starts to sweat a little."

Dingo snapped his fingers. "By God, that's right! Every time I get a haircut it gives me fits." He tugged at the druggist's sleeve again. "Let me have a pair of scissors, Fred. Turn around, Dandy. You need a trim anyway."

McGee clapped his hat firmly on his head. "I don't want you butcherin' me up!"

"I'd use horsehair if I was you, Dingo," the druggist advised. "And I don't think your horse'll be as vain as Dandy here."

"I'll just borrow these scissors for awhile then," Dingo said.

"Here," the druggist said, producing a small

envelope. "Now cut the hair short. The shorter the better."

We followed The Dingo Kid back to the street and he went to his horse and was barbering away, with Dandy McGee catching the tiny hairs and passing them to me; I was holding the envelope.

When a man said, "What you doin' there, Dingo?" we all looked up. He stood on the boardwalk, big, with a star pinned to his mackinaw. He stepped down and went under the hitchrail to see better. "Going to salt somebody's blankets?"

Dandy sniggered. "Sad-eye's longjohns."

The sheriff smiled, like a man will when he's seen most everything and finds hardly anything really amusing. "I saw him go into Grady's for his fall bath and tonic."

"Yeah, we know," Dandy said and gave me some more hair. "Is that enough, Buster?"

"You'll have to be the judge of that," I said.

The sheriff was looking at me, yet he didn't seem to be paying any particular attention. I folded the envelope and put it in my coat pocket.

The Dingo Kid said, "You get any new dodgers on me, Shaw? Oh, 'scuse me to hell. Buster, this is Shaw Buckner, the sheriff. Buster signed on this spring."

We shook hands and he appraised me openly; I suppose it was a habit formed in his work. "Like the high country?"

"It's new to me. But I'm getting along."

"Good," Shaw Buckner said. "No, Dingo, there's nothing new since that last one I showed you a year ago."

"Aw, it's those danged Arizona sheriffs; they just never forget," The Dingo Kid said, shaking his head. "And I didn't get much off that stage either." He looked at McGee. "How much was it, Dandy?"

"About fifty apiece, as I recollect," McGee said. "Cheap people ride those stages. Makes a man feel so sorry he almost ups and digs into his own pocket for a contribution."

"You stick with beef work around here," Shaw said, and under his friendliness, his open manner, there lay a dangerous core of stern commandments and a devotion to duty that wouldn't be put aside in consideration of friendship. He nodded to me and walked on and The Dingo Kid motioned for us to go on to Grady's barbershop.

"Nice fella, Shaw," Dandy McGee said. "Ain't that so, Dingo?"

"Nice when he ain't after you."

We stopped outside the barbershop and Dingo peered inside. Then he drew us into a huddle. "He's in the chair now, gettin' all curried and combed. Tell you what. Dandy and me'll go in and strike up a conversation. Then you come in a minute later, Buster, and buy a bath."

49

"I don't see how that's—"

"Now you just listen to me. Sad-eye keeps a suit of clothes in Grady's back room. Yeah, that's a fact. Yeller checks, spats and all. He bought it from the Granger's Supply House last spring when he took to wooin' the widow. Now you know what to do when you get there."

I knew and now I didn't want to, but the boat had shoved away from the bank and it was in the current and I didn't know how to paddle it back.

The Dingo Kid gave me a slap on the arm and he and Dandy McGee went inside. I heard them whoop and laugh and I waited a decent interval, then went inside. Sad-eye was in the chair and the barber was putting fragrant oil on his hair, parting it precisely down the middle and combing it toward both ears. Even his mustache had been trimmed and his sideburns were razored to an edge. His cheeks glistened.

The barber said, "You're behind these gentlemen."

"I—ah—wondered if I could buy a bath?"

"Two bits," he said. "Carry your own water. Two buckets of cold and one of hot. Got Sapolio, Pear's, White Rose, and Fairy Soap. Take your pick, a nickel each."

"Well, as long as it gets me clean, I don't care which—"

He tossed a bar to me and I almost didn't catch it. "Pear's. Got a delightful fragrance that lingers for hours," he said, combing and brushing away, his full attention on his customer.

I went into the back room. There was a huge stove going and two huge copper tubs of water steamed away on it. The wash tub was wooden, large enough for any man, and there was a sign over the stove.

BATHERS—
WHEN YOU TAKE BUCKET OF HOT WATER, POUR IN ONE BUCKET OF COLD. WATCH THE SPLASHING. FEED WOOD TO STOVE WHEN FIRE IS LOW.
THANK YOU
ELWOOD GRADY, Prop.
Grady's Tonsorial & Bath Parlor

There were towels; at first I thought they were horse blankets cut up for they were rough and heavy. I took one, and the community wash cloth; there was a rack containing brushes for the elbows and knees where a cowboy's grime was pretty well worked in, and a brush for the hands and another for the back, and a very small one for those who thought to brush their teeth, natural grown or store bought.

I found the closet where Sad-eye kept his suit and when I opened the door I saw his underwear hanging there. My conscience made me hesitate, but only for a moment; I spread the longjohns on the floor, opened front and fly and sprinkled in the hair where it would do the most good.

Then I hung them back, closed the closet door, and was taking off my own clothes when Sad-eye Nolan came in. I filled the tub with my three buckets full; it really wasn't much water.

Sad-eye said, "Why don't I add my three? I'll use the water after you."

Aware of how gamy a man can get after going a summer without a bath, other than the few times he swims a creek or goes into a waterhole, I hesitated.

"With six buckets it'll only get half as dirty, won't it?"

Such logic is not meant to be argued with, so I had my bath while Sad-eye laid out his soaps and pomades. He had a perfume, and three different soaps, and some lotion; I didn't know what he intended to do with that.

He undressed and then tied a towel around his neck. When he saw me watching him, he grinned and said, "Don't want to ruin that nice stinkum-poo the barber put on me. Besides, it's the way a gentleman bathes. Charlie Hatch said so." He showed me his lotions. "This is a skin tonic. Charlie got it for me in Billings. A man my age has to watch his wrinkles, you know."

I got out of the tub and started to dry off and he tested the water with his toe, then got in, sighing heavily. After I dressed, I went out and found Dandy McGee and The Dingo Kid holding up a building wall.

Immediately they collared me. "How did it go?" "You didn't have any trouble, did you?"

I fended them off. "He'll itch where he don't dare scratch."

They thought this was hilarious and I'm sure they conjured up bright images of Sad-eye Nolan, his ardor interrupted by the torment of his itching. Both of them clasped their stomachs and leaned against the hitchrail and The Dingo Kid laughed so hard he just let himself dangle over it, arms and legs limp. Dandy McGee sat on the edge of the boardwalk and kicked his heels and finally he rolled into the gutter and really didn't care, he was laughing so hard.

Charlie Hatch came out of the hotel and from his vantage view from the porch he saw this and threaded his way through the traffic and came over.

"What's the matter with them? They get some of the dentist's laughing gas?"

I explained the whole thing and as I talked he went, "Haha," and as I got deeper into the subject he said, "Hohohohoho," and finally, when he had it all, he was going, "HAHAHAHAHAHAHA!"

"This won't be funny to Sad-eye," I said seriously.

"Then what'd you do it for? Come on, tell me. You know better, Buster. What did you do it for?"

" 'Cause it's going to be funny, I guess," I said, and felt that it was a pretty lame excuse.

"You seen any of the other Broken T riders in town?"

I shook my head. "Been too busy, Charlie."

"I've got to find 'em and let 'em in on this," he said, starting off down the street. "They'll be sore as hell if they miss it."

He went on and The Dingo Kid straightened himself out and wiped his eyes on his neckerchief. He hammered Dandy McGee on the back and got him squared away. "Buster, Sad-eye usually goes over to the widow Mersey's house around four. That ain't far off. You meet us at the courthouse about five. It'll be dark then."

"All right," I said and went down the street to the store. I bought a can of peaches and leaned against the counter, eating them. The old fellow who waited on me didn't pay much attention to me, but there was a young woman waiting counter and she looked at me once or twice.

She was in her early twenties, fair and almost blond and she had a nice face and clear, gray eyes and somehow she didn't make me nervous. When I finished with the peaches she came down the counter and took the empty can and tossed it into a box under the counter which held other tin cans.

She smiled and said, "Peaches, pears, applesauce, you name it and sooner or later you'll develop a hunger for it. I guess that's from going from spring to fall on S.B. stew and mountain oysters." She turned to a shelf and handed me a

54

flat can of sardines. "Try these. There's a key on the bottom of the can. Help yourself to the crackers. If you like 'em you owe me eight cents."

Before I could thank her she walked away to wait on a woman who had come in with a shopping basket. I unwound the lid and speared the sardines with my knife and they were delicious with soda crackers. The owner of the store happened to come by on some errand; he stopped, whipped the knife across the horn cheese twice and shoved the slices toward me, then winked and went on.

When I was through I waited until the girl was free; I paid her for the sardines and she rang it up. "What's your name?" she asked.

"Buster Mills."

"Tess O'Shanessy," she said, and offered me her hand. "I know every rider on Broken T, Buster, and I didn't want you to be the exception." Then her smile broadened and she snapped her fingers. "The banjo player! Charlie told me about you."

"Are you a friend of Charlie's?"

Her laughter was a good sound. "You ask Charlie."

"I just may do that," I said. "And thank you for your kindness."

It was getting dark rapidly and I left the store and walked west toward the courthouse. When I came to the hotel hitchrail I untied my horse and led him on to the stable which was on the south side, on one of the short streets at right angles to the main drag. For fifty cents he got grain and a stall for the night and I went on to meet The Dingo Kid and Dandy McGee.

They were there, sitting straddle-legged on the Civil War cannon. Dandy McGee threw away his cigaret and said, "For Christ's sake, Buster, he went by fifteen minutes ago. You don't want to miss anything, do you?"

"He sure was elegant in that checkered suit," Dingo said. "I used to wear a suit like that in Sidney. Had a diamond stickpin too, but one night I got blotto in a grog shop and wound up shanghaied for the grain trade."

"Now," Dandy McGee said, "is no time to tell us the hardships you have endured, Dingo. Besides, a man ought to be drunk before he listens to sad stories."

The Dingo Kid got off the cannon, flipped his cigaret into the street and we walked the three blocks over to where the widow Mersey lived.

It was quite dark by the time we got there. She had a nice, salt-box house built of sawed lumber, which put her down right away as a widow who was fairly well off. Everyone just couldn't afford sawed lumber.

There was a fence around the lawn, and good trees, and a profusion of heavy bushes along the parlor wall, by the windows. We went over the fence just in case the gate squeaked and made it across the yard to the bushes.

When I drew near I could make out Charlie Hatch crouched there, and at least eight or ten other Broken T riders. Charlie put his finger to his lips to keep us quiet and there was a bit of crowding and shoving until we got a good place, and both The Dingo Kid and Dandy McGee thought this was deserved, for after all, it was their idea.

We could hear the soft strains of a well-played pump organ and I looked in through the lace curtains. Sad-eye was perched on the edge of his chair, tea cup and saucer in one hand and a cake plate in the other, smiling, nodding his well-groomed head to the music.

It hadn't started yet.

4

THE WIDOW Mersey finished her song at the pump organ and turned on the swivel stool to face Sad-eye Nolan. I judged her to be forty, or a year or so beyond. She was a well-proportioned woman with gray hair and a rather prominent chin. Her dress was dark velvet, and there was a brooch at the throat and ruffles at each sleeve cuff.

"Would you like more sugar in your tea, Arthur?"

There was a stir and a muted snigger in the bushes; Arthur was a name we had never known to call him and some of them repeated it like it was the funniest thing they'd ever heard.

"Oh, no," Sad-eye said. "This is just fine, Julia."

She clasped her hands together and rubbed her thumbs. "I—I suppose you'll be gone all winter."

"May get to town," he said. There was no way to get rid of the tea or cake except to eat it, and he placed the saucer on his knee and drank the tea first. "Depends on where I am, Julia. If I'm at line camp, why I'm just stuck there the winter."

Again that silence.

"That must be terribly lonely, Arthur."

He bobbed his head and someone in the bushes whispered something and Charlie Hatch slapped him across the shoulders with his hat and the man fell silent.

Sad-eye squirmed in his chair and rolled his shoulders as though his suit didn't fit quite right. He ate some of the cake and put the plate aside. "I've worked cattle all my life, Julia. To most people that ain't much."

"Don't apologize for it, Arthur."

"Ain't," Sad-eye said. "But at times like this a man wishes he was somethin' more." He waved his hands aimlessly and squirmed some more.

"If you're uncomfortable on that chair, Arthur, we could move to the sofa. Walter always liked the—" She stopped talking and looked at her hands; it was a moment of acute distress for her.

"He was a good man," Sad-eye said. "Knew him when I seen him."

"I—I didn't mean to bring him up, Arthur."

"Oh, it's all right," he put in quickly, and ran a finger under his collar. Then he put his hand under his coat as though to scratch an armpit, thought better of it and put his hands on his knees and clamped them there.

"He was a great loss to me," Julia said softly. "I was young when I married, Arthur, a giddy girl with silly notions. He was an older, more stable man. Very proper in every way." She looked at him carefully. "Are you sure you wouldn't like to sit somewhere else? That chair has a spring in it that isn't tied properly and—"

"I'm all right," Sad-eye said. He let a moment of silence hang there. "I got near five hundred dollars in the bank, Julia." He studied her, then he grew embarrassed. "I guess that ain't really much at all."

Again a long run of silence, then Julia said, "Arthur, do you like me?"

"Yes, I do. Yes, I—I wouldn't be comin' to see you if I didn't have intentions." He shifted and crossed one leg over the other and found no relief and put it down again. "I'm fifty years old, Julia. Done beef work all my life. Never had a woman to care for. Never had one that cared for me." He shrugged and twitched. "Figures right enough. Never had a home, 'cept the brand I worked for.

Can't say that I ever settled down, 'cept when I started with Broken T eight years ago." He brushed carefully at his parted hair and fluffed his mustache with a forefinger. "I've done my drinkin' and bayin' at the moon, Julia. It's all behind me and I'm a settled-down man, ready to do right by a woman."

"You're a good man, Arthur," Julia said. "I've never heard a soul speak bad of you."

He nodded, not wanting to look at her. His hands were again capping his knees and his fingers would twitch as he fought his discomfort. Then I noticed that no one in the bushes was sniggering or elbowing anyone.

"I'd have to go on cowboyin'," Sad-eye said. "Nothin' else I can do, Julia." He must have realized that he had skipped quite a bit and he started to get up, not knowing how to go on.

Quickly the widow got up and went to him, pushing him back in the chair. She sat on the floor near his feet and looked up at him and said, "Arthur, we could work it out somehow, if we wanted to."

I thought she was going to cry, but I didn't have a chance to find out because Charlie Hatch touched me and nodded, indicating that he wanted us to leave. He had to slap one or two with his hat to get them to move but we left the yard, skipped over the fence and stood in the dark street.

The Dingo Kid said, "I need a drink."

It gave us all something to do and we went to the main street and Monihan's; it was the nearest. Then we lined up at the bar and stood there as though we'd lost our last friend.

Dandy McGee said, "How in hell did we know he was going to propose?" He wiped a hand across his mouth. "The old sonofabitch, I didn't know he was serious."

Charlie Hatch said, "It sure was funny the way he squirmed, wasn't it?" I looked quickly at him to see whether or not he was serious. "You know, what he had on his mind made him uneasy enough, didn't it? Then those horsehairs in his drawers. It sure was funny."

Dingo said, "Aw, Charlie, why don't you shut up?"

One of the men down the bar said, "You think she'll turn him down, Charlie?"

"Why don't you go back and find out?"

Dandy McGee said, "It made me uneasy, watchin' through the window. I just never seen Sad-eye like that. You know, he was always a man who'd say, 'What the hell,' if somethin' didn't work out for him, but doggone if he didn't look like he was just about to stop breathin' if she'd—" He stopped talking and looked up and down the bar. "Ain't you fellas interested in what I've got to say?"

"We saw it," one man said and passed the bottle down to refill the glasses. I passed it up; one drink was all I cared for and that was my social drink to keep feelings from being hurt.

"Aw, shit," The Dingo Kid said flatly, "he's got no business wantin' to get married. What the hell's he going to do, come to town two, maybe three times a year and spend a day with his wife? You think she's going to move into some log shack on the range?"

I said, "Dingo, what Sad-eye ought to do is to turn all his problems over to you."

He looked at me, half resentful. "What the hell do you think he's going to do then?"

"He'll work things out for himself, Dingo. People always do."

Charlie Hatch was leaning against the bar, not saying much. A man down at the end said, "Hell, he may not get hitched to her at all you know." He tossed off his drink and slapped the bar. "I'm goin' back and have another look-see."

"I wouldn't do that," I said evenly, and the man stopped and looked at me.

"Is that an order or somethin'?"

"Just a good idea," Charlie Hatch put in. "Simmer down, Rags. We're all feelin' a little ashamed and wonderin' who we can blame for it." He smiled to ease the pressure off everyone. "Now why don't we just go and enjoy ourselves, huh?" He tossed some money on the bar. "Have one on me but be able to sit a horse tomorrow."

He went out and I hung around a few more

minutes to be polite, then I left and walked up and down the street, looking in the windows. There was a bakery farther down and I bought some doughnuts in a sack and I ate them while I cruised around. Up one side and down the other, slowly, with time to kill, no place to go, and nothing to do, I made a slow turn at the end, then started back and did it all over again, hoping that something would happen that was interesting enough to stop and watch. Quite a few riders were in town, some with horses wearing the Box O brand; they were from Canby Childress' ranch, some twenty miles to the east.

On Saturday night things would liven up a bit because the farmers came in then, with their women and kids and there'd be a big dance at the Odd Fellows Hall, but this wasn't Saturday night; it was a week night in the fall when shipping was done and people were beginning to button down for the winter.

I didn't see Sheriff Shaw Buckner sidle up to me; he was a quiet man, full of surprises. Before I knew it he was there, saying, "First time in Miles City, huh, Buster?"

"That's right, sheriff."

"Nice little town," Buckner said. "Growing every year. It'll last." He looked at me carefully and spent a moment lighting his cigar. "Figure you'll stay in this part of the country, Buster?"

"A year or two anyway. Hard to say."

"No sense of going back unless a man's just got to. A lot of country up here, Buster. People don't bother us much. You know the kind I mean?"

"I'm not sure," I said.

"Want to walk down to my office? Kind of cold just standin' around out here."

"Sheriff, is that an official invitation?"

"Just thought it would be better if we talked there," Shaw Buckner said. "What do you say?"

"If I was to cut and run—"

"There wouldn't be any need for that," Buckner said quickly.

And not much use either, I figured, so I turned with him and we walked to the courthouse square. The sheriff's office and jail was the whole basement floor of the courthouse, and it wasn't exactly a basement because half of it was above ground.

A stove pushed out heat and he offered me a chair and a cigar, which I didn't much care for but took to be polite. "Maybe you've been wondering how come I'm friendly with the Dingo Kid and Dandy McGee when there's posters out on 'em and rewards in Arizona and New Mexico." He shrugged. "We get a few of the wild ones here. Some of 'em turn out to be damned mean and a lot worse than their reputation." He rolled his cigar around in his mouth a bit. "A couple of 'em I had to shoot before it was over and done with." Then he leaned forward and planted his elbows on the desk top. "Buster, you want to tell me what happened in Texas?"

I hesitated and he waited, then he opened his desk drawer and laid a poster out. There I was, a drawing of course, but close enough, and a description, my name, and a reward of five hundred dollars.

"What do you want me to say, sheriff?"

Shaw Buckner took the dodger back and closed the drawer. "Why didn't you change your name, Buster?"

"It's the only one I've got. Am I arrested?"

"No," Buckner said. "But I think I've got a right to know what happened. That's a privately printed dodger and a privately subscribed reward, Buster." He tipped back in his chair and studied me; it was my move and I decided to make it right out.

"It says there I attacked a woman, sheriff."

He arched an eyebrow. "Did you?"

"No."

He smiled. "That's what Charlie Hatch said when I asked him."

It was good to know someone had faith for there had been times when I was sure that every hand was against me. "Well, when I got out of the state police in '82 I took to farming in the Mexican section of Tascosa. Nice little place. Ninety acres. Raised sheep and chickens, preached on Sunday and played my banjo on Saturday night."

"And everybody had you put down as a happy nigger," Buckner said.

"That's right."

"Family?"

I nodded. "Wife and two little girls." I rubbed my hands together and shook my head; I knew it would be hard to make him understand, and maybe he wouldn't. A lot of people just don't care to.

He said, "Buster, what do you know about me?"

"I know you're the sheriff."

"Do you know how I got to be sheriff? I'll tell you. I drifted up from Arizona after the army trouble with the Apaches. Some money in my pockets, but not enough. No man really has enough, I guess. Well, I landed here with a little and no prospect for more. It was about this time of the year and there was no hiring and everyone was expecting it to snow any time and close the country up until spring." He paused to rekindle his cigar. "Well, I took one look at the bank and wondered why I shouldn't stick it up and run with the money because winter was coming on and I didn't think anyone could chase me as hard as I ran." Shaw Buckner chuckled. "Well, I hung around town for a week, trying to decide on the perfect time to do it and the first snow came and I still hadn't moved. Then when I couldn't put it off no longer I got my horse saddled and grub packed and started for the bank. Right up main street, about opposite of the barbershop I heard two shots, then three fellas ran out of the bank, carrying bags. So I unlimbered my six shooter and we had a shoot out then and there. One dropped right off, then I was winged and fell, but I got the second one as he started to mount. The third one got away and a posse was organized and he didn't get twenty miles. So laying in the doc's bed with a bullet in my side I figured that's about as far as I'd have got too."

"You sure don't strike me as no bank robber, sheriff."

He laughed. "I was a desperate man, or thought I was, Buster. The upshot of it was I was offered the job of city marshal and seventeen months later I ran for sheriff."

"I see what you're trying to tell me, that desperation depends on a lot of different things and what's a desperate situation for one man is nothing to another."

"That's what I'm saying."

"Sure, but you never robbed the bank and you weren't even accused of it."

"No, but I told them what my intentions had been. Ask anyone who knows me and they'll tell you that Shaw Buckner started out to rob the bank." He looked at me carefully. "Now I'm a good listener, Buster. You're an intelligent man with schooling. Give me credit for havin' some sense."

He was right. A man can't clap a lid on his past because he's lived and left marks for other men to see. I dropped my cigar butt into the spittoon and stretched my legs. "There was this woman who lived near the edge of town, sheriff. She didn't work in a "house" or anything, but I guess everyone knew that she was kept by a man; he had money and a wife but he kept her just the same. It isn't uncommon. I'd been helping some friends make adobe brick and it was dark when I started for home, just walking along and strumming my banjo. Ahead I could see lights from her parlor, coming through the curtains, then I heard her yell and a man cuss and I could make her out, dashing around the porch like she was being chased. So I ran to her fence, jumped over it and the man lit out through her tomato patch; I could smell them long afterward. You know how they are when they're disturbed. She was laying on the porch like she'd fainted and I was bending down to see if I could help her when I heard people running from town. It was no place for me so I lit out and it wasn't until I was a block away that I'd realized I'd left my banjo behind."

"Did you go home? Tell your wife?"

I shook my head. "There wasn't time, sheriff. For three days I hid out on the prairie and finally I stole a canteen and made it into Colorado. In time I caught a train into Wyoming, worked off a mule and kept moving north. Then the mule played out and Charlie Hatch found me sitting on the bank of the Powder."

Shaw Buckner said, "I guess they'd have lynched you sure if you'd hung around. She'd have lied to protect the man, or it was a chance you couldn't have afforded to take." He opened the desk drawer again and took out the dodger, then scratched a match and held it until it was burned. The last piece he stamped out with his boot. "Now there's as clean a slate as a man could want, Buster."

"But you told Charlie Hatch you had that. Showed it to him maybe."

"Nope. I asked Charlie if he thought you could be in serious trouble with the law and he didn't reckon that you was because he hadn't seen you looking over your shoulder."

I didn't think the relief would come like it did, rushing in as some wave to pound a desolate shore and I had to wait a moment or two to get control of myself. Then I said, "Sheriff, I had Bullmoose Reilly mail some money for me. You don't suppose that can be traced?"

"Not likely," Buckner said. "Anything sent by stage is prepaid and then there's no station of origin on the package." He shook his head. "Ain't like a letter. Now that's got the postmaster's signature on it." He dug into his desk and brought out some letters he'd received from Butte and the copper mining towns. "Just my name and address.

69

Sent by stage. I'd do that if I was you, or put my writing inside the package."

"But I guess a man can't hide forever, can he? Somebody's bound to recognize me. Isn't that so?"

"Yes," Shaw Buckner admitted. "It always seems to happen. Men come and go, winter and spring. We get Texas men here. They come up to hear the coyote howl then drift back. When the time comes, you'll have to do something."

"What?"

He shrugged. "That's for you to decide, Buster."

"And I hope I never have to," I said. "Can I go now, sheriff?"

He smiled. "Don't go mad."

"I wish I knew how to say thanks," I told him.

"You behave yourself and never give me one whit of trouble and that'll be thanks enough."

I went out, buttoning my coat as I headed back toward the center of town. The Dingo Kid was riding up and down the street, sometimes going almost on the sidewalk in his search for someone, then he saw me crossing and rode my way.

"Buster, Charlie's looking for you. He's over at the store now." He reached down and we grasped wrists and I swung up behind him and we went on down the street. At the store I jumped off, sliding off the horse's rump while he found a place farther down and tied up.

Dandy McGee was inside with Charlie Hatch

and Tess O'Shanessy and a dozen other people and Dandy had my banjo.

"Here he is!"

"Hey, Buster, play something for us!"

"Now hold on," Charlie said. "We've got a special job for Buster tonight." He grabbed me with both hands and hauled me to the counter. "We're goin' to the widow Mersey's house and serenade her and Sad-eye Nolan."

I shook my head. "Oh, I don't think that's such a good idea, Charlie. Didn't we decide—"

"That's all been changed," Hatch said and everyone cheered.

I looked around. "What's everyone so danged happy about?"

"The widow and Sad-eye are gettin' married," Charlie Hatch said. "It's been all over town. Where the heck have you been anyway?"

"Well, I was over to—" I stopped. "I just didn't hear it, that's all, Charlie."

"We're goin' to throw a great big party," Hatch said. "All the arrangements are being made. Tess and some of the other ladies in town are fixin' up the food and Flynn's bringing two barrels of beer and we're goin' to have music and dancin' and whoopin' until dawn."

"On the widow's lawn?" I asked.

"Why, sure, where else?" He took me by the arm and steered me out and Dingo and Dandy McGee followed; Dandy carried my banjo. As we walked

71

along Charlie kept on talking. "I'm going to do somethin' for Sad-eye. Don't know what, but I'll think of somethin'. You know, a newly married man hadn't ought to be winterin' out in some line cabin. He ought to be home in bed keepin' his wife warm."

I tried to protest. "Charlie, I don't think we ought to bother them now. Don't you think we ought to wait and shivaree 'em good and not—"

"Aw, we'll do that too," he said, laughing. "Sad-eye came to me, Buster, and it was kind of sad. He asked me if it was all right if he got married. Can you imagine that? He wanted to know if it was all right with Broken T if he took a wife? I'll tell you, that touches you, don't it?"

We made a lot of noise going down the side street because we were picking up people, like the tail of some child's kite, and Sad-eye Nolan and the widow heard us coming and met us on the porch. It seemed to me that she was working very hard to be gay, but I think she was a little bit frightened of us; there were quite a few and all in a fun-loving mood.

Somehow it was a little too chilly for the party to be held on the lawn and everyone crowded into the house and a wagon came from Flynn's with the two barrels of beer. The widow was a little startled at that; I think she was a teetotaler.

But I've got to say right now that my worst fears were never realized for the cowboys didn't swear or gouge the furniture with their spurs and they didn't spill any beer on her rug. Tess and some other women came in a spring wagon with hot rolls and meat to make sandwiches and the party was in full swing.

And one time two men tried to get in and Charlie thought they were a little too drunk to behave themselves so he went outside and hit them and made them go on back to the saloon.

Sad-eye Nolan was having the time of his life, trying to be everywhere and he kept towing the widow around, introducing her very properly and it seemed to me that she was getting used to the noise and she began to relax a little. Tess and the other ladies helped put her at ease and where we were concerned I suppose she was like some eastern person looking at his first cattle herd and wondering where a man ever got the courage to ride a horse down among them.

Nolan was glued to her hand, patting it, talking softly in her ear, making her blush and giggle and he was the happiest man I'd ever seen.

For myself I just got a glass of beer and a sandwich and held up one of the parlor walls, pretty content to let it go at that. Then Sad-eye Nolan came my way, still smiling and polite. He said, "Julia, I want you to meet my friend, Buster. Buster, this is my future wife."

"It's indeed an honor," I said. "And I sure do admire the way you play the pump organ."

"Why, thank you. I—" She stopped and looked at me and I realized what I had said. Even Sad-eye Nolan had a pucker between his eyebrows. "My, Buster, how could you know that?" she asked.

"I—well, I saw the organ when I came in and it looked so free of dust I just figured you must play it real smartly."

It is peculiar how quickly sweat will come to the forehead.

"Would you play a duet with me?"

"Now?"

She waved her hands at the others. "Oh, music will quiet them down quicker than yelling. Come along." She gave Sad-eye's hand a pat. "Run along and enjoy yourself, Arthur. But one glass of beer, mind you. A man must show moderation and restraint."

Nolan nodded. "Yes, Julia, my love."

I figured then and there that they'd get along just fine.

5

THE WEDDING of Sad-eye Nolan and the widow Mersey was one of the nicest affairs of the fall, and certainly eclipsed—as far as attendance went—the lawn party held earlier by the banker's wife.

Charlie Hatch took care of most of the details and he decided that Sad-eye's checked suit was just a little too loud so they sent to the Grange Supply house and got a dark blue serge and Sad-eye looked very elegant.

Tess O'Shanessy handled the decorations and the invitations and such; she worked hand in glove with Charlie Hatch, and since I was detailed to run errands for the whole shebang, I got a chance to see them together and it made me wonder just what they were going to do about one another.

They got along real well.

Since the snow was due any day and winter was about to clamp down, it wasn't too practical for Sad-eye and his new wife to go chasing off someplace for a honeymoon, so they stayed in town while Charlie Hatch worked on the problem of what to do with Sad-eye.

Charlie went out to the O. B. Hardison mansion a couple of times, to talk it over, I suppose, but still he didn't say anything to anybody and we all waited for our assignments and wished he'd get at it because the weather was getting colder by the day and we wanted some time to get settled in if we were going to winter out away from the Moon Creek ranch.

Finally when it couldn't be put off any longer, Charlie Hatch had us gather around the porch of the Moon Creek headquarters and he told us what we were going to do. He had eight line camps in his division and I drew the eastern most one on Pumpkin Creek. There were five of us: Dandy

McGee, The Dingo Kid, Hardpan, and a rider I knew called Oily Swede.

They seemed mighty happy that I was going to be there and Dandy McGee made sure I brought my banjo along.

Before we go further, understand that line camp work isn't exactly like you read in cowboy stories, where the hero lays around and toasts by the fire. A man works cattle all the time, twenty-four hours a day when he rides for a brand, and line camp work is lonely and cold and a man is always out in the worst of it. Cattle tend to drift with a storm and a line camp rider is supposed to stop them from drifting, or if they do, he has to drive them back. The water holes freeze over all the time and a line camp rider has to keep them chopped open. He has to see that there's salt out and that it isn't covered up. And he may have to handfeed some of the stock that got crowded out of cover.

This is a dawn-to-dark business and when beef work is done there's wood to chop and meals to fix and just plain old living to do. So the big brands like Broken T put on enough men so that we could spell each other and didn't end up in the spring too gaunt to move.

So a week at a time one man would stay in the cabin, cutting wood and fixing the meals and taking care of the spare horses and doing all the housekeeping jobs while the other four rode. And when that was over you spent four weeks freezing in the saddle, hoping the good weather would hold.

The eastern camp was a good thirty miles from Moon Creek and we left with a string of twenty-five saddle horses and four pack horses, figuring to make an easy one day ride of it and arrive in the mid-afternoon so we could get settled in before dark.

Thirty miles doesn't sound like much and on a summer day it's a nice ride, but after the snow came and the wind stacked windrows and drifts twenty feet deep, thirty miles would be about as short as a casual ride to Baltimore, and just as handy.

We reached the line cabin and Oily Swede took care of the horses, putting them in a low-roofed barn, and by low I mean that the eaves nearly touched the ground while the ridge of the roof was very high so that snow would slide off.

I built a fire in the cast-iron stove in the cabin. It was a good-sized place, thirty by forty, with the bunks at one end but not crowded up. The other end was the kitchen with stored goods piled high, and there was a good root cellar.

As soon as I had a chance to look the place over, I saw that all the outbuildings were connected to the main cabin by a heavy rope strung from building to building; even the woodpile and well was so marked. Loops of rope hung on this trail rope and when the blizzards turned off blinding, a man could get from place to place without getting lost eight feet from the door and frozen to death.

The first snow fell in late September; it wasn't much, but it opened the door for a lot more. The Dingo Kid was the boss; it was something we all seemed to agree on without talking about it, and he had us draw straws, the longest getting first cabin duty. All the straws were of different lengths, which established the rotation line up. I was third down, which didn't bother me because I wanted to get out and get the lay of the land firmly in my mind before the worst of it hit.

The country was rough, hilly, timbered, and full of short, twisting canyons. Hardpan and I rode together and for two and three days at a time we'd stay out, until we had all the waterholes located, and knew where good shelter was for ourselves if we got caught bad and had to hole up.

Through October the snow fell intermittently but the wind stayed down and that kept the snow from drifting. Hardpan was on cabin duty and I was riding with Oily Swede; we'd been out four days and it was time for us to go in because we were out of grub and our horses were worn out.

As we crested a rise to drop into the creek bed where the cabin lay we ran across sleigh tracks.

Oily Swede looked at them for several minutes, then said, "I tink dat fuhnee."

Funny or not we went on to the cabin; the sleigh was parked outside by the door and as we turned our horses into the barn, Sad-eye Nolan came out. He whooped and we met on the path and wrestled and he threw me into a snowbank and I dragged him down with me and managed to wash his face good.

Then we went inside; he was just bubbling with talk.

"Give up cow work completely," he said boastingly. "Got a new job. Keeps me hoppin' but it suits me to a tee."

"How's married life?" Hardpan asked.

"Good," Nolan said.

"You and your wife fight?" Hardpan wanted to know.

Nolan reared back, saying, "That a question to ask a man? Ain't I got any privacy at all?" Then he smiled and shook his head. "Well, there was one time when we had words. To tell the truth, I fell off the wagon a little. She don't like hard liquor on a man's breath. I can tell you that." He laughed at the recollection. "Well, she lit into me with both feet, whippin' and spurrin'. Oh, it was some whoop-up, I tell you. Time it was through you never seen such beggin' and bawlin' and carryin' on."

"Aw," Hardpan said contritely. "You got her to cryin'. I'll bet you felt bad afterward."

"Her? Hell, it was me! Honey, I sez, I ain't askin' you to forgive me or even speak to me. Just let me live here."

After we got Hardpan quieted down, I said, "What's this job you've got, Sad-eye?"

"Supply," he said. "You know, keepin' this brand supplied is a big job. Up to now O'Shanessy's been doin' it at the store but it's a trouble to him and he'd been tryin' to get Charlie to do somethin' about it. Well, he has. The brand's bought wagons and stock and part of the old stable in town and I run it all. Winter time I use the sleigh." He looked from one to the other. "Brought you fellas some mail."

"The hell!" Hardpan said. "Who'd write to me?"

"Not you," Sad-eye said. "Letter for you, Buster." He reached inside his coat and handed it to me. I took it and held it and he said, "Ain't you goin' to read it?"

"Later," I said and put it away. "What all's new and excitin', Sad-eye?"

"My job, that's what's new and excitin'. While you're freezin' your ass off this winter I'll be spendin' half of my time in town, in my cozy bed with my cozy wife. And this summer while you're eatin' dust and cowshit I'll be ridin' up there on a wagon and tellin' swampers to work faster."

"You've gone and come up in the world," Hardpan said. "I'll take off my hat to you." And he did, bending low, bowing gracefully. "Would you accept a cup of coffee made by peasant hands?"

"Thought you'd never ask," Sad-eye said.

He was planning to stay the night and come

supper time, The Dingo Kid and Dandy McGee returned; it was quite a reunion and Sad-eye had to tell everything all over again.

"I think this was the smartest move Broken T ever made," Sad-eye said. "Instead of waitin' until spring, then havin' O'Shanessy work like hell gettin' provisions ready to haul, I'll be doin' that this winter and come the first road open, I'll start the wagons rollin'. You know how we're always out of somethin'? Well, it's my job to see that we ain't out of anythin'." He looked around and smiled. "Besides, who knows Broken T any better than I do? Why it'd only be in the worst weather that I couldn't get through if I had to, 'cause I know where the drifts buck up and where the clear patches are."

The Dingo Kid said, "Sad-eye, it looks like you're an important man now."

"I mean to earn my wages," Sad-eye said.

After supper I went to my bunk and read my letter. All along I had hoped that she wouldn't write and at the same time I had hoped that she would. A letter addressed to me was a dangerous thing, but I tried not to think of that.

Instead I lay back on the bunk and closed my eyes so I could see her clearly. We met in the summer of 1877; I was a sergeant in the Texas State Police then, doing duty at the Kiowa-Comanche reservation at Fort Reno, because the Texans didn't want us and the government

81

couldn't make up their mind what to do with us and the army wasn't so sure they wanted to transfer us into the regular line troops.

So reservation duty seemed just right. It was for me because I had time to study and the agency had a fine school.

She was Cherokee and a teacher, a year younger than I and I fell in love with her. We were married the next year and we both stayed on at the reservation for four years, until '82, when we both decided to go to Texas and farm a little. I'd saved my money and we had a baby girl to raise, so we bought a place at Tascosa.

I opened the letter and read it again.

Dear Buster:

Your package and dear letter arrived safely. I've worried myself sick, thinking that perhaps you were dead somewhere. The Wilson woman has said nothing at all; she will not speak of the incident, but I know that you would not do what Wade Hatton says. Sheriff Jim East will not issue a warrant, but it is not safe to come back because of Wade Hatton. He seems determined to kill you. We are all well and miss you and pray for you. The money was most welcome but do not deny yourself. I know it is a great risk writing to you, but I saw one of George Littlefield's riders in town and he said that he would mail the letter for me in

Ft. Bascom. As you know, he dislikes Wade Hatton and has had some trouble with him, so I decided to risk it. Know that we love and miss you.

Dawn

As I put the letter away it seemed strange that I really hadn't thought of Wade Hatton since coming on Broken T range; he was the kind of a man you could enjoy forgetting. It was difficult to say just what Hatton's line of work really was. He'd been a Texas Ranger but had been kicked out because he couldn't get along with the men he worked with. By the late seventies he'd made quite a reputation for himself as a gun fighter and gambler and he'd worked for three or four of the big Texas cow outfits including LIT and Lonestar but that didn't last and he settled in Tascosa, making his living gambling in Jim East's saloon.

Why he wanted me dead was something I couldn't understand because I'd never had trouble with him, mainly because I took care to steer clear of him. Hatton liked the women, but in Tascosa the only unattached women were the ones who came and went in the houses north of town. Of course there was Nan Wilson but she was the sole and private property of a pretty big man and I don't think anyone wanted to risk trouble by even looking sideways at her. The rest were married, and in Texas, about the worst thing you can do is to get mixed up with a married woman and get caught, and Wade Hatton hated to be caught in anything.

Well, I had the winter to think about it, and it was a long one because we didn't get our first genuine spring thaw until mid-May. But the snow didn't last long after that and the creeks ran wild and the grass came up thick and tender and it was the time of the year when the crews quit the line shack and went back to headquarters for a few days to collect their accumulated pay and spend some time in town.

We cleaned up the line shack, scrubbed it from top to bottom, cut the next winter's supply of wood and did all those little repair jobs that winter makes necessary around a place. Finally we loaded our pack horses and leading our string of saddle horses, started back to Crow Creek.

Some of the crew had already been paid off and were in town; Charlie Hatch told me that he was coming in that weekend because he'd be hiring the summer crew and he always did that at the hotel, setting his table up on the porch.

After we got paid, I waited until he was not too busy, then went to the main house and found him in his office. I sat down and said, "I've been here a year now, Charlie."

"Yes, you have."

I didn't know how to handle this so I twiddled my hat around in my hands a bit, then said,

"Charlie, if you had a man who hated you and was out to kill you, what would you do?"

"I'd get it settled one way or another, Buster. A man can get tired of looking back and thinking about a thing."

I showed him the letter my wife had written and he read it carefully then handed it back. "What's Hatton got against you?"

"Don't know, Charlie. I haven't said six words to him."

"Your wife seems damned definite about this."

I nodded. "You know, I'd like to go back to Texas, Charlie. I've got a farm there. And even if I didn't want to go back, I'd like to know that I could. Does that make sense?"

"Sure. So what are you going to do?"

After thinking about it all winter, I'd pretty well made up my mind. "The sheriff has no warrant for my arrest, Charlie. The Wilson woman made no complaint. It was just Wade Hatton who's pushed this, had those dodgers printed and sent out." I looked at my feet. "But I'm not able to face Hatton. Why, he'd draw and shoot me before I could spit."

"Yeah, that's so, if you went back to Texas."

I studied him. "What's that mean?"

He shrugged. "Was Hatton to come here, in a strange town, he'd be inclined to hesitate. It might just be the edge you'd need, Buster."

"You mean I should shoot it out with him?"

"Well, if he starts bangin' away, you wouldn't have much choice, would you?" He smiled. "But then I kind of figure you're smart enough to figure out some way to box him in. Man ain't much smarter than a steer who's run wild and you handle those well enough."

That made sense. "I'm going to send some more money home, and this time I'm going to put my name and address on the package. Hatton will find out soon enough and—"

"Aw, you can do better than that," Hatch said, dismissing the whole idea. "Goddamnit, Buster, don't sneak around. It ain't like you. Send the bastard a telegram and tell him to come and get you if he's a mind to. That'll make him think."

"You don't know Wade Hatton. He'll be here."

"So he'll be here. But you'll be waitin' and he won't be sure just what he's goin' to run into." He winked. "You think about that."

I left his office, saddled a horse and went to town that afternoon. By the time I'd had my bath, haircut, and got my change of clothes from the Chinese laundry I'd made up my mind that Charlie Hatch was right. I was through running and through hiding.

At the telegraph office I composed my wire, gave it to the man, paid for it, then walked down to the sheriff's office to tell Shaw Buckner what I'd done. He listened carefully, and nodded and agreed that it was the right thing to do.

I spent some time in Flynn's saloon and found The Dingo Kid and Dandy McGee there, playing cards. Dingo wanted to leave but he was on a winning streak so he had me sit down and play for him. For a moment there it was, a silent war between my personal objections to gambling and offending The Dingo Kid, and I played, figuring I could reconcile my decision a lot easier than he could understand my turning him down.

There were five of us at the table: Dandy McGee, two Box O riders, one of the shotgun ranchers from up north, and the gambler with his green eyeshade and celluloid sleeve protectors.

The game was stud, which ran the betting along nicely as each round was shown on the deal. I didn't bet with The Dingo Kid's nerve; it just wasn't in me to shove out a ten dollar gold piece and trust to luck. But I didn't want to break Dingo's luck either so I sat there and warred between conservatism and duty and won two hands in a row.

When a half hour passed, I said, "Where the devil did he go?"

Dandy looked at me out of the corner of his eye. "He's got a girl over at Hook-nosed Mae's place who lets him in before the store opens." He grinned. "Dingo's an old sailor and he hates a wet deck."

The others laughed but I didn't think it was funny. Finally The Dingo Kid came back and I gave him my chair; he looked at his winnings and nodded, then turned his concentration on the game.

There was no sense in hanging around so I went over to O'Shanessy's store. Sad-eye Nolan was loading wagons out in back; Tess told me this and I went through the back of the store to see him. He had a pile of boxes and barrels ten foot high stacked there, so I pitched in and helped him load the wagon.

When it was done we sat down and smoked. "Kind of hoped you'd be in town, Buster. Looked for you last week but—"

"We were just clearing out the line shack then," I said. "The roads are pretty bad."

"Always are but they'll dry out in a week or so. You goin' to play at the dance tonight?"

"Haven't been asked."

"Consider yourself been," he said. "Tell Tess. She's in charge of the orchestra. Pays two dollars."

"It isn't the money. I'd do it anyway."

"That's what I told her, but you still get the two dollars." Then he slapped me smartly on the chest. "Know what? My Julia's goin' to have a baby. Doc Springer said so." He grinned, then counted on his fingers. "In November sometime. Ain't that somethin'? Me, a daddy."

"Isn't she a little—well, along in years to have a baby, Sad-eye?"

His manner changed to worry. "Yeah, but the doc thinks she'll be all right." He picked at a sliver on one of the boxes. "Doc Springer thinks I ought to take her to Billings in the fall. Rent a house there and keep her handy at the hospital there so that when her time comes, why there won't be anything—any trouble they ain't ready to handle."

"You know what that'll cost, Sad-eye?"

He nodded. "Want her to have the best, Buster. Figure five dollars a day at the hotel for the two of us. That'd come to near three hundred dollars. Hospital and doctor, another two hundred anyway." He shook his head. "And I'd lose my wages. Nothin' to do about that." His expression was even more sad than usual. "Ain't got nearly that much, Buster. But I'll get it. You can figure on that. My Julia's going to have her baby just jimdandy."

We let that subject drop and talked of other things, then I left him because he had his work to finish before supper. Before leaving the store I spoke to Tess O'Shanessy and she told me to be at the Odd Fellows Hall before eight o'clock.

At the hotel, Charlie Hatch and Bullmoose Reilly were at their table, hiring on the summer crew. I stood nearby and watched, and there were a few that I recognized, having seen them the summer before, but most of them were strangers and would stay.

Working for a small outfit, a man furnished his own gear and generally his own string of saddle horses, but that wasn't practical on a ranch as big as Broken T. They owned everything except your personal clothes and saddle, and some of the older hands had even let the saddle go and used one belonging to the ranch.

This way the brand was bound to attract some real down-an-outers who'd lost everything for one reason or another. They took me when I had about walked out my boots and myself too.

So it was up to Charlie Hatch and Bullmoose Reilly to cull these men as they stepped up to the table to sign on. I would say that nearly a hundred were going to be hired, and they all weren't familiar with beef work. You could see soft hands and youngsters still in their teens, tired of pa's heavy hand or some fancied hardship at home. Out in the world for the first time and finding it a big, rough place with little sympathy to spare.

It was interesting to watch Charlie Hatch talk to these young fellows because he had a way about him that let them know he was the boss and wouldn't take anything from anyone, yet he let them know that he was a man of sympathy, who could understand a hungry belly and an empty pocket.

He signed on some of these that I'd have turned away. They could be something another man would have to carry on his back until they caught on and if they didn't work out a rider could be saddled with a partner who wasn't worth a damned thing.

But it was a chance you took and most of the time it worked out, and those times it didn't you tried to forget about as quickly as possible.

There were a few in line who seemed pretty hip-heavy with weapons and Charlie Hatch always told them that pistols and the like had to be put away while on Broken T land. Some agreed and were signed on and a few were so proud or so sure that they would be struck down for their reputation should they ever shed their gunbelt that they turned away from the job.

Jim Candless and Andy Birch came to town and joined Reilly and Hatch on the porch, for some of these men would go into their divisions and according to the policy they were permitted to choose, like kids getting up a sandlot baseball team, the most valuable players being chosen first.

It was a good way, I thought, because it let everyone know who had the reputation for being a top hand and established a sort of ascendency among the riders so that when one was put in charge of some detail there wouldn't be any argument about it.

Of course the men who had stayed on through the winter didn't have to go through this; their place was already established and they were like homesteaders who were doing a good job of proving up.

It made me feel good to be one of those men, but then, I'd been feeling good ever since I'd come into this high country.

6

A LITTLE after seven o'clock I took my banjo and went over to the Odd Fellows Hall, hoping that the other musicians would be there so we could tune up and practice a little. The piano player was a man called Knuckles, and he played regularly at Flynn's, the liveliest saloon in town. I knew him to wave at; we turned and about that time two farmers came in carrying fiddle cases. Knuckles introduced me, and before we could play anything, a guitar player and a drummer showed up. That was all and we tuned to the piano and began to play.

There was no written music of course; none of us could read notes anyway. We all played by ear but music is a logical, mathematical thing, following rigid rules and since our ears knew the rules, we had no difficulty at all working together. The dance caller was a cowboy from Box O, and around eight o'clock people began to drift in, rapidly filling the hall.

The festivities began, and at one o'clock in the morning we were still playing although the families had pretty much thinned out, leaving the single men to whoop it up and finish off that last jug.

Finally Knuckles decided that they'd had enough and we stopped playing and put away our instruments. We went to a room adjacent to the dance hall where Tess and a dozen other women were cleaning up the food tables. Knuckles and I wanted to help but they wouldn't hear of it and made us sit down and eat.

Charlie Hatch came in and went to work, helping Tess wash the dishes; it was a thing that most men wouldn't do but it didn't matter a whoop to Charlie. Shaw Buckner kept cruising in and out of the place; he'd had a busy night, breaking up a few fights and taking some of the loud mouths outside to cool off. He handled his job very efficiently. From the band stand you could see everything and I enjoyed watching him work because he was a rough, thorough man and not mean at all.

Buckner sat down at the table where Knuckles and I were enjoying fried chicken; he cuffed his hat back and said, "It's amazing how much better a band sounds with a banjo, huh, Knuckles?"

"That's a fact," he said, smiling. "In another five or six years, when he learns how to play that thing, it'll sound a lot better. How 'bout that, Buster?"

"That's about right," I said. "Maybe then we'll

get a piano player who doesn't sound like he's playin' with gloves on."

Knuckles thought that was funny and it was easy to take a joke when you played as well as he did. He obviously wasn't one of those self-taught men who pounded the ivory off the keys, and he might be the one man in the band who really knew music.

So I asked him. He gave it a moment, then said, "Buster, you may not believe it, but I studied in Europe. Going to have a great career. Whiskey and women ended that for me. I couldn't leave either alone and if that wasn't bad enough I had to keep picking the wrong women. So I picked a place no one had ever heard of, Montana. The country around Butte and Bozeman was booming with the copper strike, so I went there. Drank the saloons dry and paid for it at the piano. Finally I decided I'd had enough and quit. Haven't had a drink in four years." He grinned. "Now that you stuck your nose in my business, let me ask you something, Buster."

"Sure."

"How come you don't talk like a nigger? You know, the 'yazza boss' kind."

"I guess it's because I was never in the south until I came to Texas," I said. "Grandpa Mills was a slave to a New England ship owner. My father was the personal man-servant to an English sailing master who taught him to read and write and do numbers. I never learned to talk that way because I didn't hear it. By the time I did, I'd already formed my habits." I grinned at him. "One thing I did find out right away in Texas was that the most unpopular thing around was a black man with an education."

"Did you ever try to play Beethoven in a saloon?" Knuckles said.

Shaw Buckner slapped the table and started to get up. "Well, I'm going to try and get some sleep. Tomorrow the cattlemen will start arriving for the Association meeting. And things turn off lively since most of 'em consider themselves lords of all they survey and act like it most of the time."

I hadn't heard anything about it, which was not surprising because these matters weren't discussed among hands at all; it was none of their business. Buckner left and then Charlie and Tess came out of the kitchen; he was helping her on with her coat. She stopped at the table and gave us two dollars apiece and Knuckles said, "Now you know you don't have to do that."

"Yes, but some of the others need the money, Knuckles. And it's the deal, see. So shut up."

He laughed and pocketed the two dollars.

Charlie reached across the table and put his hand on my head, shaking it. "See me at the hotel in the morning. Nine o'clock."

I looked up, surprised. "I thought I was going back to Crow Creek—"

"You come to the hotel," he said and left with Tess O'Shanessy.

"I wonder what that's about?" I said, feeling a nudge of worry.

When I finished eating I took my plate and cup into the kitchen where the dish washers were finishing the last of the job, then got my banjo and walked toward the stable. The loft was full of clean hay so I spread my blankets and rolled in; it was cheaper than the hotel and to me a lot more comfortable.

When I woke the next morning it was sunup, so I washed at the pump, and went down to the restaurant for breakfast, then got a shave at Loch Angevine's barbershop before going to the hotel. I was early, but I intended to be, and I sat in the lobby and read the Billings paper until the wall clock said one minute to nine. Then I asked the clerk for Charlie Hatch's room number and went up the stairs.

He had two connecting rooms on the front and I knocked; he opened the door immediately and I stepped inside, hat in hand. Charlie was with another man, a large, white-haired man in a corduroy coat.

He introduced me to O. B. Hardison and I took the hand he offered; he had a grip like a saddlemaker's vise.

Charlie Hatch said, "This is the man I've been telling you about, O. B."

Hardison looked at me; he took me apart with his eyes. I found him impressive in appearance, a man of sixty, strongly built with thick shoulders and a small waist. His face was heavy-boned and deeply lined and in contrast to his white hair his mustache and eyebrows were thick and dark.

He motioned to a writing desk. "Sit down, Buster. Now you're a man asking for a job. I'm the head of the school board and you want a job teaching the first eight grades. Write a letter to me."

I wasn't sure what he was up to, but I took off my coat, sat down and dipped the pen into the ink pot. Hardison drew Charlie Hatch to one side and they talked in subdued tones so as not to bother me. I wrote for several minutes, blotted the ink, then handed the letter to O. B. Hardison.

He said, "That's a good, clear hand, Buster." He read it twice, then laid it on the table. "All right, Buster, sit down. Want a drink?" I shook my head. "I suppose you know that I'm the head of the Cattle Association."

"No, I only know what Charlie tells me."

"Well, it doesn't matter. I *am* the head of the Cattle Association, and tomorrow, and perhaps the rest of the week while we are meeting, we'll decide how the spring roundup will be conducted, who'll be boss of what, and so forth" He smiled. "You still don't see how this has anything to do with you."

"No, sir, I don't."

"Buster, we always have men who join because they have to, but they never intended to get along when they joined. We always have a problem there and we have to handle it."

I said, "The name Simon Boxley wouldn't come to mind, would it?"

Charlie Hatch laughed and O. B. Hardison nodded. "Boxley's got to straighten up or go, and I don't think he'll change his ways. This year I'm putting Charlie Hatch up for referee, northern division. I've made some inquiries to members and I think, with the exception of Boxley, he'll receive favorable vote. But that'll cause trouble, Buster. Can you see that? The Boxley tribe will paw and stamp their feet and they'll make trouble just to make Charlie look bad. I'm counting on them doing just that and it'll give me an excuse to take them before the committee and have them thrown out of the association." He paused to light his pipe. "It's my thinking that Charlie's going to be in some danger, but I reckon he can handle it. A brand referee ain't the most popular of men, but he's a necessity. However, I don't want him working alone and I don't want him takin' his attention off his work. So I asked Charlie to recommend a man he could trust, a man with enough schoolin' to keep the referee books and write reports. He said he'd take you, Buster."

"That was flattering," I said.

"You stick close to Charlie," Hardison said

flatly. "I mean watch his back. The Boxley tribe aren't to be fooled with."

"From what I've seen, I'd say that was a fact." I looked at O. B. Hardison. "What was the letter for?"

"As soon as Simon Boxley finds out you're keeping the referee book, he'll claim you can't read and write. But I've got a letter, haven't I? And a good letter." He winked. "Try to cover all bets, Buster."

"I see what you mean."

Charlie Hatch said, "Buster, you still got that pistol The Dingo Kid gave you?"

I nodded. "In my saddlebag down at the stable."

"Get yourself a belt and holster for it," Charlie said. "Sometimes a referee's decision is only as good as the man behind it." He dug into his pocket and gave me a ten dollar gold piece. "Get a couple boxes of shells and do some practicin' a mile or so out of town."

"You don't want me to go back to Moon Creek just yet?"

"You can go back when I do, when the meeting's over," Charlie Hatch said, smiling. "You got anything against a week in town?"

"Not at all," I said and turned to the door. Hardison was unfolding a map and laying it out on the big table and I closed the door and went on down to the street.

I walked to the stable, got the pistol out of the

saddlebag, stuck it back in the right hand chap pocket, then walked over one street to a small saddlemaker's shop. He was alone, working on a carved headstall and he put this down when I stepped up to the counter.

I showed him the pistol. "Like to have a holster for this."

"Four inch barrel. That's more a pocket pistol than anything." Then he saw my chaps. "Sew something onto the leg just above the pocket; that's my recommendation. Want something with a flap?"

I shook my head. "I'd like to be able to get at it in a hurry if I had to."

He nodded and dug into a box under his counter, coming up with an old cavalry flap holster. With his head knife he cut this open, measured by eye, trimmed, folded it around the .44, then sewed a back piece on it. He wanted me to put on the chaps so he could get the holster positioned, then I took them off and he sewed the holster in place, pedalling away at his treadle machine. Then he punched a hole in the chaps, pushed through a piece of leather with a slot in it; this could be slipped over the hammer as a safety strap.

His charge was two and a half and I paid him. As he dropped the money in his apron pocket, he said, "Do you know anything about draw and shoot?"

"No." Then I thought of The Dingo Kid. "But I know somebody who can teach me."

"Let me see those chaps again." He took them and sewed a dozen cartridge loops on the belt. "No charge," he said and went back to his lacing job.

I bought the cartridges at the store and Tess told me she'd seen The Dingo Kid and Dandy McGee going down the street not a half hour ago, so I made the rounds of the saloons and found them playing cards. Both of them were looking for something to do and as soon as I told them what I wanted, we left, got our horses and rode west of town about a mile.

We tied the horses in a brushy thicket and I began my training in pistol shooting. It wasn't difficult, the way Dingo and Dandy taught it, kind of like pointing your forefinger. We worked with unloaded guns until I got the hang of reaching, cocking as I drew, and snapping the hammer and when I felt sure of myself, Dingo put in a shell, spun the cylinder and told me to go ahead. I didn't know whether or not the live shell was coming up, but it didn't bother me; I drew and the gun recoiled and the bullet went just about where I wanted it to go.

"You're on your own now," The Dingo Kid said and he and Dandy got their horses and went back to town.

I stayed until nearly dark, shot up a half a box of shells, then rode back. The stable man lent me some oil and his cleaning rod and I cleaned the pistol, put it away, then went to the restaurant for supper.

Afterward I thought I'd cruise around, smoke a cigaret, then get to bed early, only I'd just stepped out of the restaurant, pausing on the boardwalk to make my cigaret, when I heard someone say, "Ain't that the nigger that was with Charlie Hatch?"

My head came around and I saw two men standing in front of the hardware store; just enough light came through the front window for me to recognize two of the Boxley brothers. They stepped my way and the older one laughed.

"We didn't get much of a chance to talk when you was in Crow Rock."

"I didn't know we had anything to say."

They looked at each other and the younger said, "Oh, he's a smart one, Art. Nobody's ever taught him."

"We could," Art Boxley said.

"Right here?"

"Why not?" he said.

Across the street, on the hotel porch, someone stopped and looked our way but I dared not take my attention away from the Boxley brothers. Art started to take off his coat, then stopped when Charlie Hatch came into his line of vision. Charlie said, "A little trouble here, Buster?"

"Working up to that," I said.

"What do you want to do about it?" Charlie asked pleasantly.

I hesitated. The Dingo Kid and Dandy McGee were coming down the walk and several people were following them. They arrived and stood around and by the time I'd made up my mind, fifteen people stood there.

"I don't think I ought to let it go," I said.

Arthur Boxley said, "For Christ's sake, we were just havin' a little fun!"

"Looks like you're still goin' to have it," Charlie Hatch said. "Which one do you want first?"

"The older," I said and shed my coat. Dandy McGee caught it and folded it neatly over his arm. There was a disturbance at the edge of the crowd and Simon Boxley came bulling through.

"What the hell's goin' on here?" he wanted to know.

"Your two boys want a fight," Charlie Hatch said. "So they're goin' to get it. And you're goin' to stay out of it, ain't you, old man?"

"Sure he is," Dingo said, moving to stand behind him. He looked at me. "Whenever you want, Buster."

Arthur looked at his father. "Pa?"

"Shut your mouth and fight!" the old man snapped.

"Hell, we was just havin' fun," Arthur said. "Ain't that right, Roy?" He took his brother by the arm, determined to drag him into it.

"Fight!" the old man roared and would have hit his son if The Dingo Kid hadn't restrained him.

Charlie Hatch said, "I guess there's nothing to this, Buster."

"Maybe they'd feel braver if I took them two at a time," I said, realizing that this was dangerous, yet I took the risk. They had been ready to jump me, perhaps thinking that I'd have backed away from it, but now they had backed down and everyone knew it. Fighting now wouldn't change their minds because everyone would think that they had been pushed into it.

Charlie Hatch said, "Let the old man go, Dingo. He can take the boys over to the store and get them some warm milk and put 'em to bed." He looked at me. "How about comin' over to the hotel, Buster. I've got some things I want to talk over with you."

"All right," I said. Then I reached out, grabbed Arthur Boxley and before he could brace himself I flung him into the hitchrail, bending him way over backwards. "Mister, stay clear of me. You understand that? I won't be fun any time. You got that clear?" I waited until he nodded, then I let him go and pushed through the crowd with Charlie Hatch.

Shaw Buckner was standing in the street; I hadn't seen him at all until then. He smiled and said, "When a man ain't got the guts to get you from the front, he sometimes has enough to try it from behind. Hope you remember that, Buster."

"I won't forget it," I promised, and went to the hotel with Charlie.

In his room he took me over to the table where he had maps spread. Already lines and letters and pencil markings covered them. He pointed with a pencil. "Our division will be six roundup wagons and nearly two hundred men. Jim Candless is division boss this year and we're starting over in Rosebud County and moving northeast along the Porcupine and crossing the Big Dry to the north. Likely we'll swing as far north as Fort Peck, then east to cross the Redwater." He traced the route with his pencil and already it had covered two hundred miles. "Then southward across the Yellowstone and then west to the Powder and Andy Birch's headquarters at Locate." He tossed the pencil down. "There'll be at least eighteen brands involved, and a lot of shotgun outfits that will move in and out of the drive. It'll be a rustler's paradise, Buster, with all those brands bunched up and the drive moving every day. A good man could cut out a dozen calves, push them out of our way then swing back and hold them and the chances are good that he'd get away with it."

He offered me a cigar and a brandbook. "Smoke the cigar and memorize the brands and the names of the owners. Have you ever worked with a referee before?"

I shook my head.

"Most of the stock is slick-eared; we don't go

much for ear marking here. And the rustlers are too smart to doctor a brand, so they hair-brand calves, just burning enough of the hair off so that it looks all right under casual inspection. Some of the shotgun outfits have written to the Association, claiming that Simon Boxley's been doing some hair-branding. We're liable to run into some disputes over it."

"If it don't turn out to be more than that fracas on the street—"

"That was a quarrel," Charlie interrupted. "An argument over stock is an argument over dollars and now and then men reach for a rifle." He puffed on his cigar. "We'll be on the go from dawn to dark and since we won't have a camp, we'll eat, sleep, and take horses from any outfit we come across, keepin' an account, of course, of where we picked up the horse and dropped it. They'll have to be returned in the summer by the wranglers. A referee's word is binding; all the outfits have agreed to that when they heard the articles, and signed them. The shotgun outfits, even though they aren't in the Association, agree to the referee's decision. Fact is, they give us less trouble than Simon Boxley."

"How do you handle these shotgun outfits, Charlie? Do you gather their stock along with the rest?"

"Hell no. They round up for themselves. But suppose you're chasin' some brush snake with your brand on him and he moves in with a bunch carryin' a brand belonging to a shotgun outfit. The critter's calmed down and you can handle him now, so you chouse the whole bunch along and cut the herd later. Some get mixed up that way but if a critter isn't carryin' an Association brand, you leave him alone."

"When do you want me to have these brands memorized?"

"Do it tonight, if you can. The meeting will start tomorrow morning. First item of business will be to approve the roundup plan and the articles. O. B. figured that'll all be over by noon. Comes afternoon and it'll be voting on the roundup foremen and referees. When your name comes up, O. B. wants to be able to say that you know all the brands. Make sense?"

"I wouldn't argue with it."

He grinned and slapped me on the head. "Had supper?"

"At the restaurant."

"You stay here then. I'm goin' down to the store and help Tess close up."

"Can't she do that by herself?"

"I wouldn't let her," Charlie Hatch said. "If a man was the marryin' kind, she'd make a good wife."

"Seems to me she'd be that even if a man wasn't the marryin' kind."

"She don't take me seriously though," Charlie said.

"You really believe that?"

"Why, sure. She knows I just fun around." He frowned. "Aw, you just like to see me worry. I'd never go too far. Not old Charlie Hatch. I've been around the park, friend. Keep 'em laughin', that's my motto."

"What do you do after you close the store?" I asked, smiling. "You walk her home, slow and easy, and then she fixes you a cup of coffee and maybe cuts you a piece of pie or cake she's baked. Then you tell her that she's a good cook and good looking to boot. And afterward you sit and chew the fat and kiss her goodnight."

"So?"

"So who's fooling who?"

He scratched the back of his head. "That's not like sayin' a lot of things you don't mean."

"You'll say 'em and you'll mean 'em. You've already got a ring in your nose."

He put his hand up to feel and I laughed; he didn't think it was very funny. "Listen, I've got too much sense to get married. Tess knows that. We just have a good time together."

I kept shaking my head. "Charlic, you'll be just like Sad-eye Nolan. It's the way man goes, Charlie. It's the way he's made. You're having fun and that's all right but one of these times she's going to tell you that you could go on having fun and getting married too and you won't have an argument for that."

"Boy, you sure know how to take the joy out of life," he said, and clapped on his hat. "You care to make a bet that I don't get led to the altar?"

"Nope, because I can already hear the wedding bells."

"Read your damned book," he said, and went out.

7

SPRING IN Montana really begins around June, and spring is roundup time, and many armies have taken to the field with less preparation than these cow outfits. In all, eighteen brands were represented, and the men combined, unified, split into divisions, each following a planned route and headed for a fixed destination.

Charlie Hatch and I knew the roundup plan; it was necessary for us to know the schedule of movement and where herds were to be held. Our camp was on the Little Dry, in Garfield County and our division ranged thirty miles west along the Big Dry to a place on the Redwater an equal distance to the east.

The western division was refereed by a gunfighter named Gunnison, and the eastern was handled by Bullmoose Reilly.

Charlie Hatch and I left Miles City with a string of saddle horses and two pack horses and made a two day push to cover seventy-five miles. We established a camp and spent an easy day or two, then broke camp and saddled up.

We knew where the first gather was going to be made to the west and pointed ourselves that way. Most of the time we stayed to the high ground because it was important for us to see as much as possible.

Toward evening we found the roundup wagon, turned our spare horses into the remuda and from there on in would be picking our saddle ponies from whatever camp we came across. The section boss was a man I'd never seen before, but we found The Dingo Kid and Dandy McGee in this crew, and a couple of riders from Box O that Charlie Hatch knew.

No one had had any trouble, and that figured because the roundup had just gotten started and tempers weren't up yet. Give it another week or ten days when everyone was getting worn to a frazzle and the food was beginning to taste bad and then there'd be a lot of slicker-waving to hail a referee.

"None of the Boxley hands are in this camp," The Dingo Kid said to me. "And I'm happy to say that."

"It's going to be a nice friendly affair," Dandy agreed.

We were stretched out by the fire, the last of the coffee in our cups. Dandy and The Dingo Kid had night herd in another hour and were waiting to be called.

"It's kind of lonesome without Sad-eye around," Dingo said.

"Yeah," McGee agreed. "Everything's goin' to hell. Raunchy is cookin' for some outfit from Dawson County, and Hardpan is working western division."

"I hear Oily Swede got thrown in with Leaning S, and he never liked the Boxley brand a-tall," Dingo said. He fell silent for a moment. "We saw Sad-eye when we were in town, Buster. He's worried some about payin' for that kid."

"He'll work it out somehow," I told them, and pretended that I believed that. I dug into my jumper pocket for a map and consulted it. "Doc Springer's going to be at the junction of the Big Dry and Little Dry in five days. Maybe if you get a chance, ask him how she is."

"I'll have a toothache for him to look at," The Dingo Kid said.

I put the map away. Roundup time is a dangerous time, and men get hurt. The Association made arrangements for the doctor and sometimes a dentist to be at certain camps at certain times, and injured men and the sick men are taken there to be tended. It was an improvement on the camp cook doubling as bone-setter and home remedy dispenser.

"He likes bein' married," Dandy said. "You can tell. The bastard is even putting on weight."

The Dingo Kid looked at me. "You hear any more from your wife, Buster?"

"No. I sent her some more money and a letter though. One of these days—" I let the rest trail off and Dandy McGee glanced at me.

Dingo said, "Buster, if there's anything you can't handle alone, you know you only have to whistle."

"Sure, but I'd have to take care of this myself. It's one of those things." I sat up to roll a cigaret. "His name's Wade Hatton and he'll be lookin' for me before the summer's over because I told him where to find me."

Dingo raised an eyebrow. "That what the six-shooter practice was all about?"

"Part of it. Hatton's got a reputation and a hate for me. I'd like to know why."

"Sometimes there isn't a reason," McGee said. "And it may be that it's better if there isn't a reason." A rider came into the camp and put up his horse. McGee and The Dingo Kid got up. "See you around, Buster."

They left the fire and I rolled into my blankets. In the morning when I got up they were already gone. Charlie Hatch and I ate, saddled and moved north until noon, then swung down into a long valley where a herd was being gathered and cut. There was a brand dispute and Charlie Hatch settled it after examining the brand carefully. They were all haired over and personally I would have had difficulty making the decision; it took a man who not only knew the brand, but could often identify the man who had handled the iron. Each man has his own touch with an iron. A real expert will burn in the brand just enough to make a good scar while someone with a heavy hand will seriously blotch the brand. Steadiness is important, and iron heat is critical. Some men work with the iron a little too cold while others keep it too hot.

All these things were taken into consideration and were the basis for Charlie Hatch's ruling.

We moved from herd to herd, eating where we found a camp, changing horses so often I lost track of them. And all the time I kept thinking of the men riding bog and gathering weak stock and doing calf work on the home range and somehow wishing I were there.

I kept books constantly, making rough tallies and making entries when Charlie Hatch had to settle a matter of brand dispute. And we kept working north and east and I noticed that we were picking up a lot of Leaning S stock, the Boxley brand.

And Boxley trouble.

We were in McCone County, on the Redwater and we had come onto this camp around noon and were pretty well tied into a plate of beans when a Walking A rider came into the camp in a hurry. He didn't want coffee or beans; he wanted Charlie Hatch because there was trouble cooking.

We were already saddled so it was just a matter of dropping the beans and mounting up. The Walking A rider gave us the details: he and two others had leg-tied two brush snakes and were in the process of horning another to a tree when Arthur Boxley and four others came in from the northeast. Immediately there was a hassle over the steers; their brands were haired over and they were as wild as you'd find.

The Walking A riders were not going to be buffaloed out of the steers because they'd read the brands as theirs, but Arthur threw down on them with a rifle and that's where it stood, Arthur claiming the steers were Leaning S and ready to back it up with lead.

We reached the clearing in a half hour and it was as the rider had said; Arthur and his men were there and Arthur had command of the whole situation with his Winchester. Charlie Hatch rode in, dismounted and said, "Put that away, Arthur."

"If it goes my way I will," he said.

"It goes the way I say," Charlie told him.

I opened my record book and put the pencil behind my ear and took care to hold the book with my left hand, leaving my right free to draw my pistol if it became necessary. Charlie Hatch made a close examination of the steer the cowboys had horn tied to the tree. He took his time, then straightened and said, "Walking A."

"Walking A, hell!" Arthur snapped. "The first man who puts a rope to that steer gets hurt."

I wrote Hatch's decision down and noted the time and the number of men present. One of the Walking A riders looked at me. "That official?"

I nodded and he shook out a loop and started to make a hobble.

My instinct was to watch him, but I looked at Charlie Hatch and Arthur Boxley; Arthur still held the rifle and he swung it to cover the Walking A cowboy. I saw the muscles in the back of his hand tighten and opened my mouth to yell a warning, but I didn't have to.

Charlie's pistol came up and out of the holster and he rolled the hammer under his thumb and the bullet hit Arthur just an instant before he fired. The impact spun him and he dropped the rifle and fell to his knees. He looked stupidly at Charlie Hatch, then sagged forward and fell on his face.

One of the Boxley hands reached for a rifle in a saddle scabbard and I said, "Now don't do that, mister."

It held him. The sudden death held them all and only Charlie Hatch moved. He rolled Arthur over, then got the slicker off his saddle and put it over him.

"I'll rule these brands now," he said and took his time; he was very calm, very deliberate, and ruled two of the steers to Leaning S.

It was all very stupid and needless for had

Arthur waited, he would have claimed two of the steers. Now he was dead.

I closed the book and put it in the saddlebag. Charlie Hatch said, "Load him on his horse. I'll take him in to your main camp if you'll tell me where it is."

No one argued with him because no one wanted the job of taking Simon Boxley's son in across his horse. The Walking A men claimed their steer and drove it on and after Arthur had been tied across his saddle, Hatch mounted and I followed suit.

We left the clearing, traveling in a southerly direction and after an hour we came to Leaning S; the camp was not far and we could see the smoke from the cook fire.

Simon Boxley had a large tent pitched; it was common for the camp to pitch tents, even for the riders. They saw us coming with a dead man and by the time we approached the fire, the old man came out of his tent, saw his son and ran to him with a cry, flinging his arms around Arthur's head.

I was going to dismount, but Charlie Hatch shook his head. He said, "Sayin' I'm sorry this had to happen isn't much, Simon, but the boy was just determined to shoot somebody with his rifle."

The old man looked up. "Who shot him?"

"I did," Charlie Hatch said. "Because I had to."

"You lie!"

"You know I don't."

He faced Simon Boxley but I kept kneeing my

horse around and sat my saddle with my hand on the butt of my pistol, watching them all, watching Charlie Hatch's back. I knew they wouldn't be after justice because Arthur wasn't that well liked, but they were all men of hot tempers and an explosion was likely.

Yet none wanted to start anything; even the old man was restrained by caution. He said, "Broken T doesn't rule the world. I'm going to have a warrant sworn out."

"That's a good idea," Hatch admitted. "The law should handle this. I'll be easy to find." He turned his horse and rode out and I waited a moment, then followed him. After we were clear of the camp he let the strain in his face show through and his hands shook when he rolled a cigaret. "It's always bad," he said. "Never gets better either." Then he struck the saddle horn with his fist. "That stupid bastard, wavin' his rifle around! The first time in my whole life that I have to pull a gun on a man and I go and kill him."

"Charlie, there wasn't anything else you could do. I saw his eyes just before you shot. He was going to shoot that cowboy."

"Sure, sure, but why couldn't I have winged him? I'm a lousy damned shot anyway so I pointed at the broadest part of him. Dingo or Dandy McGee would have busted his arm but I had to hit him in the chest." He drew deep on the cigaret as though the smoke could numb him a little. "This may be my last roundup as boss or anything else. If O. B. thinks this shouldn't have happened or could have been avoided—"

"O. B. wasn't there, Charlie, so how could he know? I don't care what comes out at the coroner's inquest. You had a little part of a second to make up your mind. And you did right. I don't see how it can be said otherwise."

"We'll see," Charlie Hatch said.

It doesn't take long for the word to get around that there's been a shooting and Charlie Hatch had me write up a full report of it and he had a rider take it to the nearest telegraph office at Locate. Shaw Buckner was notified and O. B. Hardison, and Hardison would provide the sheriff with the roundup schedule so that he could meet Charlie Hatch and the others involved in four or five days.

All this may sound a little involved, but you didn't just up and shoot another man, regardless of the circumstances, without an official investigation. It may be more romantic to dispatch one's enemies with a six-shooter, then hie to the nearest saloon and wash away any regrets with red-eye, but it isn't very practical. In no time at all there'd be a lot of dead people around and no one responsible for them.

The next few days, Charlie Hatch and I worked the hills and holding pastures and valley places and he was very indrawn and quiet. Not morose, or sullen. Just thoughtful.

We worked around toward O'Fallon Creek; it took us six days and there at the main camp we found O. B. Hardison and Shaw Buckner waiting for us. Hardison had already sent word out that he wanted the Walking A riders who were witnesses, and the Leaning S men who were there to come in to testify at the hearing. Dr. Paul Springer, who was also the coroner, arrived in his buggy to conduct the hearing.

Simon Boxley and his two remaining sons arrived. A large tent had been pitched and we gathered inside until the hearing began, then Dr. Springer called witnesses one at a time, Charlie Hatch being first. We remained outside, around a fire where the coffee pot was kept bubbling and finally Charlie came out, put his hat on, and motioned for me to go on in.

The flies were droning thick and the tent was getting hot and pretty thick with cigar smoke. Dr. Springer, O. B. Hardison, and the sheriff sat at a camp table. I sat down facing them.

"Your name?" Springer asked.

"Buster Mills."

He consulted my record book, then looked at me. "Is this a true and accurate account of events leading up to the shooting?"

"Yes, sir. Up to, including, and afterward."

"On this piece of paper, draw the positions of

the principals." He shoved a pencil and a large pad toward me and I went to the table. I drew the tree where the steer had been horn-tied, and I drew the other two steers that had been hobbled. "This is where Arthur Boxley was standing," I said, making a circle and putting his initials in it. "Almost directly behind him stood another Leaning S rider. The other two were in this direction, about ten yards. They were still mounted." I placed a diamond to represent Charlie Hatch, a square to show where I had been, and X's to indicate the Walking A hands. "As you can see, Charlie was standing nearly between myself and Arthur Boxley. My main attention was on the Leaning S riders."

"Why?" Springer asked.

"Because we'd been told there was trouble and that Arthur was holding a rifle on the Walking A hands. The dispute was over three steers. Walking A claimed them and Arthur said they were clearly Leaning S." I made a pencil sketch of Leaning S: Ƨ Then I drew a Walking A over it: ⅄ "As you can see, sir, it sure wouldn't pass as a blotted brand, but on a brush snake that was haired over, especially on a brand that was put on light, it would be hard to tell. There wasn't any doubt that there was a legitimate dispute, but the Walking A men didn't like to see it settled at the point of a rifle."

"Thank you," Springer said. "Sheriff?"

"I have a few questions," Shaw Buckner said. "Was Arthur still flourishin' his rifle when you and Charlie arrived?"

"Yes."

"What did Charlie say?"

I tried to recall exactly. "Put that thing up, or words to that effect."

"And Arthur said?"

"If this goes my way I will, or to that effect."

"Any other conversation?"

"Nope. Charlie inspected the first steer, the one that had been horn-tied to the tree and ruled Walking A. Then Arthur lost his temper, swore a little, and said that any man that put a rope on that steer was going to get hurt. One of the Walking A riders asked me if the ruling was official and since I'd already entered it in the book, I allowed that it was and I shook out a loop. It was then that Arthur turned his gun on him."

"And at that point," O. B. Hardison said, "Charlie Hatch drew and shot him?"

"Yes, sir."

Springer said, "Did Arthur fire his rifle?"

"Yes, sir, just a split instant after Charlie fired. The bullet hit the tree that the steer was tied to. I guess it missed the Walking A man by a good ten inches."

Springer looked left and right. "Any further questions, gentlemen?"

O. B. Hardison said, "Buster, in the light of what

you know about Arthur Boxley, and the way he always tries to run a bluff, do you think he meant to shoot that cowboy?"

"He had his rifle cocked and pointed. It's like climbing on a strange horse; you don't know whether or not he'll pitch until he does. So you kind of figure he will and be ready for it." I shook my head. "I had my hand on my gun and I was ready to use it, if that means anything at all."

"It'll be considered," Dr. Springer said and told me I could leave.

All that afternoon the questioning went on and the witnesses were heard and finally it was all over and we were invited to crowd into the tent. Simon Boxley was there with his dour expression; his two sons waited outside. Springer cleared his throat and we were still.

"It is the decision of this inquest, based on consideration of the facts, that the shooting of Arthur Boxley was justified because of the attitude and conduct of the deceased prior to the shooting. This hearing is terminated and the matter is closed."

Simon Boxley looked stunned. "Is that all?" he yelled.

Springer looked at him. "I want you to get something straight, Mr. Boxley. Your son lost his judgment, his temper, and his life. That's pretty damned expensive considering that two of the steers in question were ruled in your favor. I sincerely suggest that no further trouble be made over this."

"If there's settlin' to be done," Boxley declared, "then I'll do it my way in my own good time." He turned and walked out and a moment later he and his sons left the camp.

Charlie Hatch was relieved of official responsibility, but he had killed a man in a quarrel over a steer and he wasn't going to forget it. He seemed to want to be by himself so I didn't pester him. Instead I went over for a plate of grub and a cup of coffee. Dr. Paul Springer found me there; he helped himself and sat down beside me.

"Have you seen your two friends lately?"

"You mean Dingo and Dandy?" I shook my head. "Not for ten days anyway."

"They talked to me when I was at the Redwater camp. They're worried about Sad-eye Nolan's wife."

"I guess that's so, doc. I'm some concerned about her myself. She's no young girl."

"I tried to assure them that everything will be all right. We'll get her to the hospital early and—"

"Did they talk to you about how much this was going to cost?"

"Yes, that was their main point," Springer said. "It's going to cost a lot of money. Of course, I can waive my fee, but that's only a small part of the bill." He shook his head. "She's going to need special care, Buster. No way around it."

"I see." I didn't have any money so there was no use in my worrying about it. We talked about the roundup; he had a lot of cow sense and wanted to know if the rustlers had been busy. There was some talk of it around, but no one had been caught at it, and personally I figured that the winter had taken quite a few head of stock and the rustlers—if there were any—were getting the blame for it.

When I finished my meal I went to Charlie Hatch, thinking that we'd be leaving, but he wanted to spend the night and leave in the morning, which was all right with me since I could do with the sleep.

The roundup wouldn't last more than another week and it was a relief to me because I'd seen a lot of camps, worn out a lot of horses, and looked at a lot of cattle and it would be good to get on home range again.

I rolled into my blankets at the edge of camp and slept soundly until someone shook me awake. It was pitch black and then a match flared and I saw Oily Swede and Hardpan kneeling there.

"Hunted all over hell for you," Hardpan said. "Can't you sleep in a tent like other folks?"

"What time is it?"

"What do you care? After midnight. Have you seen Dingo or Dandy lately?"

"No. What's the matter?"

Hardpan snorted through his nose. "We joined up with 'em six or seven days ago. Working high north after bunch quitters. They'd light out, be gone all day and never show hide nor hair. Five days ago they lit out and didn't come back. Oily and I sat on this as long as we could, Buster, but in another week we'll be startin' back and they're bound to be missed."

I threw off my blankets and sat up, tugging on my boots. "Any ideas, Hardpan?"

"Hate to talk about 'em. Been bad enough just thinkin' 'em."

"Poor time to be having secrets," I said. "What do you think?"

He hesitated. "Dingo and Dandy are doin' a little rustlin'." He looked at Oily Swede. "There ain't no other reason, Buster. They never gathered as much stock as the rest of us. Now and then they'd show up chousin' some brush snake, but never calves. Swede and I think they've been herdin' beef into some small box canyon they found and holdin' them there. Course, now, that they've been gone five days straight, we figure they're drivin' someplace for a quick sale."

"How many head do you think they have?"

Hardpan shrugged. "Twenty maybe. It's about all they could handle. You got to help us, Buster."

"To do what?"

"To get them calves back before Dingo and Dandy sell 'em. I like 'em both too well to see 'em hung."

"Did you tell Charlie?"

125

"Christ, no!"

"He's got to be told, Hardpan. You know that."

"Just couldn't bring myself to do it, that's all. So I come to you." He looked at me intently, staring in the darkness. "Can you tell him?"

"I don't see that I have any choice," I said.

8

WHEN I woke Charlie Hatch I identified myself and he raised the chimney on a lantern and lit it. Without making it fancy or letting anything hang in doubt I told him exactly what Hardpan and Oily Swede said, and the conclusions they had drawn.

He thought about it, his expression grave as he kept running his hand over his chin, scraping the whiskers as though they itched. Finally he said, "First thing, let's keep this to ourselves until we're sure. No sense in startin' a rumor that'll spread like a brush fire." He rolled a cigaret. "Seems pretty foolish to go rammin' around tonight. Come morning, the four of us will just up and leave camp. We'll see if we can't cut some sign."

"All right," I said, then: "Charlie, what are you going to do?"

"Find 'em first. And if it's true, I'll arrest 'em."

"You think Dingo and Dandy will—"

He shook his head. "I don't know. Find that out, I guess."

He blew out the lamp and settled down and I

126

went back to my own blankets but I couldn't sleep. Oily Swede and Hardpan had rolled in near my bedding but we didn't talk.

There wasn't anything to talk about.

When a man works for a cow outfit, he makes friends and they are more than acquaintances, the kind of people a city man knows and invites over once in a while. We ate the same dust and ran the same risks and the same rain wet us all and the cold chilled each man alike. And in the nature of our work, we worked together, helping each other. It threw a man in with another man, day and night, week after week, and you got to be friends. Good friends. The kind of friends that didn't ask whether it was right or wrong.

Then something like this happened and you had to choose between the friend and the brand; it was like choosing between brother and mother and at best it tore a man's feelings and left him less than he had been before.

Before dawn I was up and over to the cook fire and the coffee pot and Charlie Hatch was already there, along with Hardpan and Oily Swede. There were others getting up but we formed a small island to one side and everyone let us alone.

The daylight marched on, brightening the sky with flaming color, then Oily Swede nudged me and drew my attention to the north side of camp. Dandy McGee was dismounting by the horse herd; he dropped the reins and came into the camp, switching his head from side to side as though he were looking for someone.

Then he saw us and increased his pace. He grabbed Charlie Hatch by the arm and looked around to see who was in earshot. When he spoke he kept his voice low. "I'll make this quick, Charlie. Dingo and I have spent ten days makin' contact with the rustlers. We cinched it when we drove eleven head of calves into the canyon where they're holdin' a herd. That convinced 'em that Dingo and I were tired of workin' for wages." He looked around again. "One thing I want to get settled: Does the Association still pay five hundred dollars for information leadin' to the arrest and conviction—"

"Yes," Charlie Hatch said.

"Then Dingo and I claim it. We can take you to where the herd's held and give you names."

"Give me names then," Charlie invited.

"Arthur Boxley. He was there better'n a week ago but we ain't seen him since. The old man's been there too, and his youngest boy. There's Indian Sam and three others from shotgun outfits."

"Have the Boxleys been drivin' in unbranded stock?"

"Well, sure, what did you think? There must be three hundred head held there now."

"Where's their market?"

"They drive west into the mining country. No one asks questions there."

"Where's Dingo now?"

"With them. We couldn't both leave."

"I see," Charlie Hatch said. "Tell me one thing, Dandy. How come you did this?"

"We wanted the money."

"Hell, I understand that, but what for?"

"To pay Sad-eye Nolan's hospital bill when it comes time for his wife to have the baby," Dandy McGee said.

I saw the tightness leave Charlie Hatch's face; he believed this, as I believed it because it was exactly the thing The Dingo Kid and Dandy McGee would do for a friend, and even though they were implicated and there would be trouble over it, I was glad they hadn't taken to robbing the stages again.

"You wait here," Charlie said and walked over to O. B. Hardison's tent and went inside.

I said, "Don't hold this against Hardpan or Oily Swede. They came to me and I went to Charlie."

Dandy McGee laughed softly. "Damn it, that's what we wanted only it looked like those two stupids weren't ever goin' to tell anybody. When it got so we couldn't wait any longer, I left camp and came here."

Charlie Hatch pushed the tent flap back and motioned for us to come on in. O. B. Hardison was pulling on his pants and hoisting his suspenders; he looked at Dandy McGee a moment then said, "I don't know whether to throw my arms around you or to kick your ass. It's for sure that we have to move and not waste time about it. Shaw Buckner's still in camp. I want him to go along; you can fill him in on the details while you're travelin'. Dandy, get the hell back but first I want you to look up old man Boxley and tell him he's needed there."

"Is he here?" Dandy asked and Hardison explained the shooting. Dandy whistled. "So that's why he didn't come back! The herd won't move without old man Boxley's say so. That's for sure."

"Where can the herd be intercepted?" Hardison asked.

Dandy scratched his head. "Well, was you to take some high ground on the west end of the Dry, you'd be bound to see us. Dingo and I will both be on the inside when the shootin' starts, so I'd appreciate it if you didn't throw any lead our way."

"All right," Hardison said. "We'll find you. Now clear out of here, but see Simon Boxley before you leave. If he wants to know why you're here, tell him you were looking for him and heard he was here." He offered his hand and a smile. "You and Dingo take care of yourselves, hear?"

"That's our intention," Dandy said and ducked out.

Hardison pulled at his lip. "How many men do you need, Charlie?"

"Well, I'll take Buster and Shaw. Dingo and

Dandy McGee will be one hell of a surprise to 'em. I guess Hardpan and Oily Swede."

Hardison nodded although I was sure that he did not agree with so light a show of force. But he had left it up to Charlie Hatch and he was not going to quarrel with the decision. "Draw rifles and ammunition out of the wagon. Pick your horses after Dandy and the Boxleys clear the camp."

After we stepped outside, Charlie Hatch told me to pick out the horses; we would take along a spare saddle horse apiece because we would want to ride hard and there would be no time to dismount and walk. And now that the roundup crews were heading in, we couldn't count on picking up spare mounts.

I was roping out what I wanted when Shaw Buckner came up, a catch rope in hand. He saw a big rangy bay that he liked and caught him and brought him over to the picket rope.

"Dandy and the Boxleys left camp," Buckner said. "I put together the bedding and some sacks of grub. They're over by the cook's wagon."

By the time we had saddled, Charlie Hatch was ready; he and Oily Swede came over, burdened with bedrolls and Hardpan carried the rifles. Charlie said, "The quicker we get out of here, the less attention we'll attract." He made a cutting motion to the west. "No sense of us all leaving together. Shaw, you and Buster light out. Wait for us. We'll catch up."

Buckner nodded, tied on his bedding and mounted; he was turning out when I swung up and followed him. I caught him just past the edge of camp and we rode for several miles without saying anything.

Finally he said, "Do you believe Dandy's story?"

"About the rustlers?"

"About collecting the reward for Sad-eye Nolan."

"Yes, I believe that. Sad-eye is a friend."

"I'd like to believe it," Buckner said. "I'd like to think that I didn't have to worry about The Dingo Kid." He shrugged. "Well, we'll see, won't we?"

He paused on some high ground and looked back, then we walked the horses for a spell and when Charlie Hatch and the other two came toward us we stopped to wait for them.

"I figure we're three days from the end of the Dry," Charlie said, his expression grave. "And I'm for campin' light and short and makin' as much time as we can. Either way, to Lewistown or Billings, they'll have to follow the canyons out of the Big Dry. You agree, Shaw?"

"I'd say that was likely."

"Then we're wastin' time," Charlie Hatch said.

It was dark when we stopped for a small fire, a plate of meat, some biscuits and coffee. Charlie Hatch picked a place in the rocks where the fire couldn't be seen and we didn't stay but a few hours. When I woke and looked at the sky I figured it to be around one or two o'clock in the morning and I felt like a man who hadn't had enough sleep.

Charlie was for moving on and we didn't argue. He led the way and we followed him, single file, not moving fast, but traveling west all the time. Come dawn we were getting into some badlands, rocky, the draws choked with brush. At sunup he stopped and we built up another small fire and we had some coffee for breakfast and nothing more during the day except biscuits and water and we ate that on the move.

That night, while we were laying out our blankets Shaw Buckner said, "It would irritate me no end if I found out that Dingo and Dandy were movin' off in some opposite direction."

"Dandy told it straight," Charlie Hatch said.

"I hope he did," Buckner said.

Doubt crept into my mind and I know that it bothered Charlie Hatch because if Dandy had drawn us on a snipe hunt while he and Dingo headed off in another direction with some stolen calves, we'd likely never catch them with the goods. We only had Dandy's word that the Boxley bunch were rustling; it could be a lie and we all wondered about it and kept our thoughts to ourselves.

The next day, Charlie Hatch was where he

wanted to be, on high ground with a good view of the Big Dry and the trail leading out of that country to the mines. He left us and was gone for several hours, then he came back and flung off and squatted on the ground.

"Been lookin' over some of the country hereabout," he said. "If they come through here, I don't think we'll stop 'em. All they'd have to do is stampede the stock and make a fight of it." He took off his hat and wiped his face with a neckerchief. "But I guess if we followed the Big Dry back and stayed to high ground we could see their dust plain enough."

"They'll be pushing pretty hard too," I said.

"That's right," Charlie agreed. "So we hit 'em while they're at night camp. I don't see any other way unless it's just get into a shootin' match that'll get half of us killed." He looked at each of us. "Agreed?"

We agreed.

Hardpan made the fire and the evening meal and we were in the saddle and moving again by dark, working northeast along the Big Dry and keeping to the high ground. I felt sure that we wouldn't spot the herd or the night camp because we'd moved twice as fast as cattle could travel and had worked around way ahead of them.

We worried away the night, a mile at a time, and it was nearly dawn when we stopped to catch a few hours' sleep. The sun, which had climbed high and hot woke us and we made some coffee. Charlie and Hardpan were away on some high rocks, having a look, but they came back, having seen nothing.

We ate some cold meat and hard biscuits, drank coffee and smoked, then Charlie wanted to be moving again so I hauled a pretty stiff carcass into the saddle.

Long about midafternoon Oily Swede saw dust and we watched it awhile, feeling that it might be some freak wind. But it hung too steady for that and we knew that underneath it was a herd of calves being hurried along.

Shaw Buckner said, "Charlie, I feel a whole lot better."

"Hell, so do I." He smiled, and again seemed to be in good spirits.

There was no need of us going farther so we dismounted and took turns watching the dust while the others slept. The herd covered a good four miles by nightfall and then we could see the cookfire glow brightly and we silently cursed the rustlers for having hot grub while we didn't dare show a match for a cigaret.

We slept until very late, almost midnight, then Charlie Hatch came around and woke us. We gathered around and he said, "They'll have two nighthawks. The rest will be in camp. That's three of the Boxleys, Dingo and Dandy and probably two more. Now the last thing we want is for that herd to stampede, which means no damned shootin'. Swede, do you and Hardpan think you can handle the nighthawks without stirrin' the dead?"

"A rock is pretty quiet," Hardpan said, "especially when swung in a sock."

"All right, but once you get those nighthawks tied up, start easin' that herd on, you understand?"

"Sure."

"It'll take us an hour to get down to the valley floor," Charlie said. "When we get there we'll give you another hour. Now move slow and careful and get those calves a mile away from camp just in case fireworks commence."

Hardpan said, "Charlie, do you want me to turn that herd so that if it does stampede it'll come smack dab back through the camp?"

"Hell," Buckner said, "we'll be caught in it."

"No," Charlie disagreed. "We'll know it's comin'. Good idea, Hardpan." He reached out and touched me. 'Buster, you look like midnight even in the sun, so I'm goin' to have you sneak in and wake Dingo and Dandy."

"They could be the nighthawks," Buckner said.

Charlie shook his head. "No, they're expectin' us and they'd get out of it some way. Shaw, you and I will follow Buster in and try to cover the others. Everyone understand?"

We all did and then it was time to mount up and begin working our way down into the valley. It

136

took time because we could make no sound; a slip would have alerted the camp and our advantage would go up in smoke.

In closer, it became obvious that the camp was on one side of the Big Dry and the herd of calves was on the other, which made it better for us. Hardpan and Oily Swede left us and crossed over; the water was low and they worked downstream, then split on the other side.

Charlie's timing began to make sense to me, now that I thought about it, for at sundown the night herd riders would begin their tour and that would last about four hours, which meant that they'd go in and wake their relief about midnight. Since we'd left the high camp about then and took an hour to work down, and then added another hour on for Hardpan and Oily to make their move, the nighthawks wouldn't think a thing of anyone approaching them on a horse; they'd just figure it was the relief coming out to start early.

But it wasn't easy, waiting and not knowing what was happening out there. If the herd was being moved it was done so slowly, so gently that we weren't aware of it, and since we heard no disturbance across the river we just had to assume that Hardpan and Oily Swede were doing what they were supposed to be doing. None of us were sleepy; that sly Charlie Hatch had pushed us until we'd been worn to a frazzle, so tired we'd shifted our sleeping to the day and now, at two in the morning, we were as awake as birds twittering on a limb.

Finally it was time for me to go and I took off my spurs so they wouldn't jingle; I kind of favored those Mexican danglers so popular in Texas and on a noisy night in town you could hear a man coming for two blocks when he wore them. I had my rifle and a full magazine and one round in the chamber with the hammer at half cock and I went on in afoot, moving like a cat across a feather tick.

The fire was out and the night was like thrown mud, but I could make out the mounds on the ground and approached one cautiously. A man snored beneath his blankets and it was a snore I had never heard before so I passed on to another.

I saw the "horse jewelry" on the hatband and recognized The Dingo Kid. Kneeling, I clamped a hand over his mouth and he came awake instantly and there was the muzzle of his .44 pressed against my breastbone. Then he put the gun away and sat up, making no sound.

He drew my head down and whispered, "Dandy," and pointed to a mound of blankets some ten yards away. I went over there and did the same thing and when I straightened I found The Dingo Kid beside me, his rifle in hand. Dandy McGee got up and made some motions with his hands, indicating which one he'd take and the one he'd picked for Dingo and myself.

We nodded and split, moving over to the men bedded down on the ground. For a moment I studied the man and then looked around. I thought I saw Charlie Hatch and Shaw Buckner moving in, but I couldn't be sure and it wasn't safe to take my attention off my work. Kneeling, I smothered the man's mouth and pressed the rifle muzzle against his temple. He gave a start, stiffened, then relaxed.

Very softly I said, "Get up." I took my hand off his mouth, snatched his pistol from his holster and put my foot on his rifle. He stood up, then on the other side of the fire there was a blow struck and a man grunted and fell over.

Another came awake and Shaw Buckner said, "Touch your gun and you're a dead man."

There was a rasp of metal as handcuffs closed shut.

Charlie Hatch threw some wood on the fire and it began to blaze and widen the circle of light. I pushed my man over and saw that it was Simon Boxley; The Dingo Kid had the young son and Charlie Hatch had knocked out the other one.

Boxley said, "What is this?" He peered around as though he couldn't see good and was trying his best to make us out. We stood there while the wood caught and the fire got bigger and brighter. Then he could make us out and his expression turned sour. "Buckner, you've got no authority in this county."

"He don't need any," Charlie Hatch said. "Bring those others over here." Then he walked around and looked at each of them carefully. "Ain't you a fine bunch? Get some rope, Dingo."

"Hell, he's with us," Boxley snapped. "Him and Dandy McGee."

"Old man," Dingo said, "I was never with you."

He got some rope and tied them hand and foot, lining them up by the fire. Simon Boxley swore and struggled and got cuffed a few times before he grew quiet. "Where's Ed and Rowdy?"

As though he had heard him, Oily Swede splashed across the river, herding the two night riders tied to the saddles. One of them had a bloody gash on his head and the other sagged in the saddle as though too sick to sit straight. Oily came up close to the fire, then said, "Aye go with Hardpan now," and rode back.

"Looks like we caught all the rabbits," Shaw Buckner said dryly.

"You caught nothing!" Boxley yelled. "By golly a man's got a right to drive his own calves to market." He jerked at the ropes. "You're rustlers, that's what you are. Every calf in that herd is wearin' a registered brand. I'll have your ass up before the Association for this!"

"Fresh brands?" Charlie Hatch asked.

"Hell, they're just scabbin'," Dingo said. "Less than a week old."

"You shut your rotten mouth!" Boxley yelled.

"I'm going to collect five hundred dollars for you," Dingo said. "You smart old bastard, walkin' big all the time, and throwin' a wide loop. You've been pickin' off calves like this for years. We all suspected it."

"Don't be so damned high yourself, Dingo! You rustled same as any of us. A good ten calves you and Dandy drove into the canyon. And don't say you didn't."

"Now I didn't intend to," Dingo admitted. "Hell, how else was we goin' to get on the high side of you?" He laughed. "Dandy and I spotted your canyon by accident, so we drove in a few head like we'd just stumbled onto it accidental like. What could you do? Let us go? You had to take us in and that's what we wanted."

"I told on you," Dandy said. "Five hundred looks good to us and that's sure a heap more'n your pelt's worth."

The old man glared. "If you think your testimony is going to hang me, by God you'll find that mine will hang you too." He looked at Shaw Buckner. "Ain't that the law?"

Buckner pursed his lips. "Charlie, he's got a point there that's going to take a judge and lawyers to straighten out."

"Aw, come on," Dingo said. "Without us you wouldn't have caught 'em and you know it."

"That's right," Charlie said. "That's a hard nut to chew without crackin', Shaw."

"True, but the question that'll have to be answered is why you boys waited so long."

"Hell, there wasn't time!" Dandy McGee said, getting disgusted with the whole thing.

The Dingo Kid asked the important question. "Sheriff, are you arrestin' Dandy and me?"

"Well, no I ain't, but I do suggest that you come back and stay in town until this thing comes to court. I don't know what the judge is going to say about it, Dingo. And I wouldn't want to guess what the county attorney will say. The whole thing seems to hinge on what your intentions were when you started putting your rope on unbranded calves."

"We told ya!" Dandy yelled.

"Now cool off," Charlie Hatch said soothingly. "We'll get it all ironed out just dandy. None of your friends are going to let you down and the Association is going to be mighty grateful. If you need a lawyer, why they've got some good ones." He turned to me. "Catch up your horse and give Oily and Hardpan a hand. We'll want to drive back come daylight."

9

WITH ROUNDUP over, shipping began and the herds were gathered, foreman and crew picked and the drive south moved, down through the North Platte country of Wyoming then southwest to the railhead at Ogden, Utah. Having been on a cattle drive once, it was not my kind of work for a man had to be fiddle-footed by nature to like it, and most of the men who went along were the drifting kind, inclined to be hard to get along with, and other than the trail boss and foremen, they were not really part of anyone's permanent crew. Some would come back and some wouldn't. No one cared either way.

Miles City was our destination, and the jail for Simon Boxley and friends. All this created quite a stir in town because rustlers didn't often get to jail. They were usually hung long before they got there.

O. B. Hardison wired for an Association attorney, and he arrived on the next stage and the county attorney was chomping the bit, eager to hold the preliminary hearing because people said that he had political ambitions and this case would attract favorable attention to himself.

The Dingo Kid and Dandy McGee were not locked up, which caused some talk, for it was no secret that they had been in the gang and were responsible for its capture. This caused a few factions to spring up. On one side there were those who felt that these two men were upright citizens and an asset to the community. On the other hand many felt that free society was no place for stage-bandits and gunmen of established reputation.

It was a debate I stayed clear of and no one tried to swing me to one side or the other and I think that was because they couldn't make up their minds. I was an associate of both Dingo and Dandy McGee, and I was also a close friend of Charlie Hatch, and I was seen several times talking with O. B. Hardison.

People were not inclined to offend O. B. Hardison when they could avoid it.

There were two letters waiting for me, both from my wife. I drew some pay, sent her some money, and a long letter and still sidestepped the issue of what I was going to do about being with my family.

The days of hanging around town waiting for things to come to a boil began to gall on me; I would rather have been working at something. I suppose Tess O'Shanessy saw this because she came up to me in the store one afternoon and said, "Buster, you look lonesome."

"Tired of loafing," I admitted.

"Charlie says it may be another three weeks before this is settled. Want a job?"

This surprised me. "Here?" I shook my head. "Some of your customers wouldn't like it."

"I didn't mean here," she said. "Come on in the back. There's coffee on and we can talk there."

I went with her and she gave me a cup and invited me to sit down and smoke if I liked. "Charlie says you're an educated man, and I can

144

see that he's right, Buster. It's a shame to waste that."

"I don't think it's wasted," I said.

"Wasted because you're not using it is what I meant. We have a good school here, Buster. Of course the kids have just started their vacation now and the teacher's gone to Arizona for the summer. What I'm trying to say is that some of the children need help. They didn't do too well and the parents don't want them to fall behind. If someone would tutor them—"

"Me?"

"Why not? There's no money connected with it. But you know how, Buster. It would just be for a half day, eight to twelve."

The idea was very appealing, but I had large reservations. "I don't think some parents would—"

"Then let their hyenas stay home," Tess snapped. "I've already talked it over with the school board and they're agreeable. What do you say, Buster? Give it a try?"

"Well, I'd have to talk to Charlie and—"

"Charlie agrees," she said, and smiled. "He didn't have a chance."

"I can see that. But O. B. Hard—"

"He agrees too."

I laughed. "Did you ever have any experience in building wild horse traps? All right, I'll do it. But if it doesn't work out—"

"We won't worry about that," she said. "You can begin in the morning."

"I'll have to get a suit of clothes."

"Why don't you look over the stock?" Tess invited. "I've talked pop into donating it to the cause."

I put my coffee cup aside and looked at her. "Will you tell me something? When are you and Charlie getting married?"

"This fall."

"Does he know it?"

"Oh, not yet. It'll be a grand affair."

I cocked an eyebrow. "You don't suppose he'll object?"

She wrinkled her nose. "Not much."

Twelve pupils ranging from eight to fifteen is not much of a class, but I was most happy with them. Each had some kind of a problem: poor grades in spelling or numbers, or their handwriting was not good. Some had difficulty in reading.

This was my first experience in teaching, but my wife, Dawn, had a diploma and she had taught school under difficult circumstances, where every student had a problem and I knew how she handled it.

Those slow in reading had their class, and at the same time those poor in writing had to copy the reading text; it was killing two birds with one stone and it worked very well. In numbers, the ones who had no problem were paired with those who did and we made a team effort of it.

To keep them from poking along I offered an inducement: Their assignments had to be completed before school was dismissed and if it took five hours, then we remained five hours. Much of their difficulty was the inability to put their minds on the business at hand, but the sunshine and the freedom of summer beckoning outside gave them the incentive and soon school was regularly dismissed an hour early.

Shaw Buckner dropped around to see me twice. An attorney had arrived from Billings to represent the Boxley faction and the judge had set the date for the preliminary hearing so that indictments could be drawn up.

I'd be called as a principal witness.

When I asked about Dingo and Dandy, Buckner said they'd gone back to the Moon Creek ranch but had been sent for and would be in town tomorrow. They were still concerned about getting the reward money for Sad-eye Nolan.

He worried a great deal, and mostly about keeping people out of trouble.

Each afternoon I would remain at the school and plan carefully my next day's work; I was inexperienced and keeping ahead of children is not a simple thing, as most parents will agree in honest moments.

It is difficult to say how much I enjoyed the job

147

of teaching; I had never suspected that it would be so rewarding, so personally satisfying and I knew that when the time came to give it up I'd be sorry that it had to end. I suppose when a man builds a bridge of impressive dimensions, or lays railroad track through mountains he feels a great sense of satisfaction. It is also satisfying to see minds grasp facts, to watch intelligence bloom.

It was a very warm summer afternoon and I had the window open, to encourage a little breeze that was stirring the trees outside. The birds were singing their best songs; they have a few for weather like that, and I was going over the reading lesson, making a list of the words that needed spelling attention. I didn't hear anyone ride up, or drive up and my first indication that anyone was there was when a woman said, "Buster Mills?"

I looked up and for a moment I didn't recognize her, then when I did I felt a sudden chill, a start, like one feels in the middle of the night when a strange sound awakens him.

She smiled at me and said, "May I come in, Buster?"

I got up and moved a chair around for her so I could sit behind the desk and look at her and yet still keep an eye on the door. In the first drawer was the pistol The Dingo Kid had given me and I kept it there always, waiting for that time when I'd have to use it against Wade Hatton.

Nan Wilson took off her hat and veil. She was thirty or so, quite striking with bold eyes and a good figure. But this was the first time I had ever seen her close. "What are you doing here, Miss Wilson?" I asked.

"I came to see you, Buster, to say that I'm sorry." She stripped off her gloves and folded them neatly. "I suppose you hate me."

"No."

"But you feel sorry for me."

"A little. But not for you. For anyone who can't call themselves their own—well, master, to use an overworked word."

"I suppose you've figured out by now why Wade hates you."

I shook my head. "He's always been a man who hates easily. I never wasted the time figuring it out."

"You saw him that night, Buster."

"I saw a man running. That was all. I didn't recognize him."

She studied her folded hands. "I see. But he couldn't take the chance. Don't you understand that?" She looked at me as though she expected me to sympathize with her, to say something, but I clung to silence, understanding that it was a strong weapon when an opponent is uncertain. "Well, I was tired of being poor, Buster. That's all there is to it. I had the looks to attract men, but they were all poor too and I didn't want that.

Then this—gentleman saw me. I knew who he was, that he was married, and that he'd stay that way."

"And you fell in love with him right away," I suggested.

"No. I never loved him, Buster. But he loved me and he bought me a house and kept me in style. I made my bargain."

"But you didn't stick to it."

She glanced at me then pulled her eyes away. "No, I just couldn't. Not after meeting Wade. Sure, he's no damned good and he chases and he gets into gun fights and someday he's going to end up face down in the street, but I love him. I couldn't say no to him."

"Wade Hatton hit you the night I was coming along the road," I said. "That didn't change anything?"

"Nothing. He always wanted me to run away with him but I knew it wouldn't work. This gentleman had money and power and he'd have just reached out and squeezed Wade and had him killed." She paused. "Do you have any cigarets?"

"I roll my own."

She shrugged. "I suppose you're already trying to figure out who the gentleman is. Or I suppose you know."

"Everyone in Tascosa knew," I said.

Her expression told me that I had shattered one

of her remaining delusions. Then she laughed briefly. "And I thought I was at least giving the impression of respectability."

"No, it was a fancy," I said. "Everyone knew who was keeping you and that you had never had a husband who died and left you money. It was never a secret for long."

"But no one ever let on."

"What reason did anyone have?"

She nodded. "I suppose that's it. No reason at all. That night of the trouble, Wade and I quarreled about my leaving. Oh, I was sharp with a dollar, Buster. Believe me, I salted plenty and it was enough to give us a start. But you know, even when you love a man you can't put aside all those greedy years and I just couldn't give up that easy money."

"Easy?"

She wouldn't look at me. "Oh, you can be so damned noble, can't you? The poor, downtrodden man with his good-good wife and scrubbed kids. What did I have?"

"What you wanted. What you bargained for," I said. "Don't cry to me. You're wasting it. I kept my mouth shut and I got out because Wade Hatton had a bunch of his cronies set to hang me. I don't owe you a thing."

"I came here to say that I was sorry I didn't speak up. But I couldn't, don't you see? If I had, Wade would be dead now."

"Yeah, and he's worth saving, isn't he?"

"To me he is." She straightened in the chair and looked at me. "That was pretty bold of you, sending him that telegram. But he had already figured out where you were after your wife sent you that letter."

"Where is Wade now?"

"At the hotel," she said. "He came in on the stage with me."

It surprised me, but did not alarm me as I thought it would, and my voice and manner were calm. "So you've given it all up for him?"

"Yes, all of it. I left a note. By the time he finds out where we went we'll be long gone from here. Wade only wants to finish his business."

"You're quite a woman," I said. "As cold and brutal as any man I've ever known. You tell me you've come to say you're sorry, and then you sit there and tell me calmly that as soon as Wade Hatton kills me you'll move on. I suppose all this will be a balm to your conscience, if you have any left."

She smiled at me and said, "Buster, I do what I do to take care of myself because no one else will ever do it for me. Wade didn't want me to see you at all but I insisted; I thought you had a right to know." She got up and put on her hat and gloves. "He'll be waiting for you up town. Don't keep him waiting long, Buster."

It angered me, her manner, as though she were

closing some business deal. I said, "I'm here. Tell him that if he wants me."

"All right, I'll tell him that," she said. "Buster, understand that there's no turning back now, for either of us. You can't run from Wade and I can't go back to Tascosa."

"Neither can I go back," I said, "because there'll always be people there who believed Wade Hatton."

"Yes. But then, I suppose no one really gets everything just the way they want it. Goodbye, Buster. And I'm sorry."

"About what?"

"Why, I think it's because we're going to have to sort of throw you away, Buster. No one really likes to do that, you know." A horseman rode up out front and stopped and for an instant my heart began to pound, then I heard Charlie Hatch speak soothingly to the horse and I relaxed.

He came in and stopped just inside the door. "Oops. Didn't know you had company, Buster."

"She was just leaving," I said, and Nan Wilson walked out with a swirl of skirts.

As she passed Charlie Hatch she stopped and looked back. "You're a friend of Buster's?"

"Yes," he said. "Aren't you?"

"They always cost too much," she said, and left.

Charlie Hatch laughed and cuffed his hat to the back of his head. "Now there goes a tough little chippie. Seems like I saw her come in on the morning stage." He frowned and snapped his fingers. "Wait a minute! She ain't part of that Texas trouble, is she?"

I nodded. "Wade Hatton was with her. He'll come here soon."

"Hell, you don't have to fight him," Charlie said. "One word to Shaw Buckner and Hatton will land in jail."

"For how long?"

"Long enough to cool him off."

"He won't cool off," I said. "I offend him, Charlie, and that's all the reason he needs. Besides, I have friends here. I like it here. This is my home now and I mean to walk about like a man, Charlie."

"Sure, I understand. But he's a gunslick, Buster. Don't forget it and give him any kind of an edge."

"No, I won't. Charlie, I can rely on you to take care of everything, can't I? I mean, my wife and kids—"

"Now don't go thinkin' like that," he snapped. He reached under his coat and handed me a .44 Colt pistol, the short-barreled model. "You stick that in your belt, out of sight. Times like this, a man can always use a spare. You've still got that other pistol, haven't you?"

I nodded. "In the desk drawer."

"Have it in your hand when he gets here," Charlie Hatch said. He reached out and grabbed my head and shook it. "Damned idiot, you stay awake now!" He grinned and went out and mounted his horse.

The schoolroom was very silent and I took the .44 Merwin-Hulbert out of the drawer, checked the loads, then cocked it and laid it on my thigh. I left Charlie's pistol in my belt, knowing that it was loaded, five shots there, ten in all.

And I wondered if I would live long enough to fire them.

It isn't a pleasant thing to know that there is a man who wants to kill you, and it is a lot more unpleasant to know that he intends to do just that. I could have summoned Shaw Buckner; it was within my legal rights, but we don't often live by legal rights alone. To go on living, to go on being respected, I had to take care of my own trouble. The men I worked with had to know that I would and could handle my own trouble. They had to know, to see my character; it had to be simply put so that they would understand it.

And that's why I sat there and waited for Wade Hatton to show up.

He came, as I knew he would, not fifteen minutes after Charlie Hatch had left. I saw his shadow an instant before he appeared in the door and I had my hand on my gun. He stopped in the doorway, as tall as I remembered, with a thin, handsome face and his pearl-handled pistol tied to his thigh.

He was smoking a cigar and kept it in his mouth

when he smiled. "Buster," he said, "I just don't feel like a lot of talk." And then his hand went down and up and even though I was prepared, I was shocked to see him pull a gun that fast. As he fired I left my chair and used the oak desk for cover; his bullet plowed a furrow across the top and made splinters fly, and I fired from around the corner.

I think I nicked him because he flinched and took a step back, firing again; I heard the bullet thud into the desk but it did not pass through. Quickly—perhaps too quickly—I rolled the hammer under my thumb, fired three more times and did not hit him, but the fusilade forced him to dodge outside.

Leaving the cover of the desk, I sprinted toward a corner and when he poked his head and shoulder around the door jam, I sighted more carefully and broke his collar bone.

He spun around and staggered a step away from the door and I threw the Merwin-Hulbert away and grabbed Charlie's pistol. I ran toward the door but stayed back, not exposing myself right away. Then I couldn't wait any longer and I jumped squarely in the doorway.

Hatton was surprised and fired too quickly; the bullet narrowly missed me and I shot again, hitting him more squarely this time. He fell in a spiral, but did not lose his gun and immediately he rolled and tried to get to his feet.

"That's enough!" I yelled but it didn't stop him.

He was swinging up his gun, more slowly now because he was hurt and there wasn't anything I could do but shoot. I took the .44 in both hands, holding it like The Dingo Kid had taught me, and slip-hammer shot it, rolling them off fast. He was pounded back, jerking, jumping and then he went limp and the pearl-handled gun fell from his fingers.

The shots had attracted a crowd and people were running toward the school and Charlie Hatch was racing Shaw Buckner to see who was going to get there first. Charlie took a look at Wade Hatton and Buckner said, "Better give me that, Buster." He took Charlie's empty pistol and turned to keep the crowd back. "That's far enough! You can't do anything here. Baldy, you and Frank hold 'em back there. Come on now, folks, don't be hard to get along with."

Charlie Hatch said, "He's sure dead, Shaw."

Nan Wilson was pushing her way through the crowd; she broke through and stopped so quickly that she staggered. She looked at Wade Hatton as though she couldn't believe it, then she looked at me and large tears formed in her eyes.

But she wiped them away and her expression hardened; there was no real regret in her. "I guess," she said, "that I'm the one who got thrown away. I can't go back, Buster. What will I do?"

"I thought you always knew what to do," I said.

She looked at Wade Hatton and shook her head.

"Next week you'll have trouble remembering his name," I told her.

She looked steadily at me. "You think I'm nothing, don't you? Well, you killed him and the law's standing right there waiting to arrest you."

"I don't have to run here," I said. "Besides, the sheriff knew why Wade came here. He knew I sent the telegram. People here know, Nan. Look around and then tell me who's the stranger, the intruder."

Her glance went to Shaw Buckner and then to Charlie Hatch. "You could have stopped it, both of you."

"Could have," Charlie said gravely. "But what for? It was Wade who wanted the settlin', wasn't it? You and Wade together?"

"Not I," Nan Wilson said quickly. "I came and warned Buster!"

"He didn't need a warning," Shaw Buckner said. "He knew what was coming. You want to pay for Wade's funeral expenses?"

"No," she said dully. "He was headed for boothill somewhere. It might as well be here."

"Well we'll take care of him then," Shaw Buckner said. "Don't you stay in town any longer than the next stage out."

She was offended and glared at him. "You'd put me on?"

"Lady, you can bet on it. We have four

prostitutes in town now and we don't need a fifth." He gave it to her like a fist in the face and her complexion went white; I think it was the first time she had ever faced the truth of anything and it was not easy for her.

Without a word she turned and the crowd kind of eased back and let her walk through; then it closed after her like water making the wake of a boat. Shaw Buckner sighed and handed the gun to Charlie Hatch. "This is yours, I guess." He looked at Wade Hatton, laying all cramped up and still, his white linen shirt soaked with blood. "You look at a man like that and it's sure a strong argument for holdin' your tongue and dyin' naturally in bed. Never saw one yet that wasn't messy and undignified as hell. It's bad, a man goin' out face down in the dirt and horse piddle. But some have just got to do it that way it seems." He turned and touched me lightly on the shoulder. "Don't go worryin' about this now, Buster. There won't be any trouble."

"What do you call this?" I asked.

He nodded. "See what you mean."

10

IT IS one thing to observe and quite another to do, and when Charlie Hatch had to pull his gun and shoot Arthur Boxley I did understand that it was something he hadn't wanted to do, and something he regretted afterward. But I did not really understand what it meant until I was forced to shoot Wade Hatton.

There are many men—I'm happy to say, the majority of men—who simply go through life without ever killing much of anything. Many of them do not hunt. And all of them do not think of the possibility of shooting another man. It just does not enter into their consideration.

Charlie Hatch was that way and so was I; even in the police service I was never called upon to point a gun at a man and pull the trigger. Somehow situations always resolved without that moment of violence.

And now, reflecting upon it, I had clung to the belief that somehow the anger of Wade Hatton would be resolved without shooting. I was wrong there and I clearly believe I shot in self-defense, yet he was dead and I had done it and then I really understood that period of withdrawn silence Charlie Hatch had gone through, snapping out of it only when the business of the rustlers came up and brushed it back into the file corner of his mind.

The hearing did it for me.

Judge Little was presiding; he had come in from Billings to hear the case through. This may sound a bit confusing, bringing in a judge from another county, and Shaw Buckner, the sheriff of Custer County making the arrest in a county four times

160

removed. Actually, the counties of Montana were laid out, as they were in Texas, with many of them unimproved, or undeveloped, and that being the case, they were officially served by law enforcement officers from the nearest improved county. As an example, Tascosa, Texas, where I hailed from, was in Oldham County, and Jim East served as the sheriff, with Temple Houston as county attorney. Only there were ten unorganized counties surrounding it and Oldham furnished whatever law and order they had, which meant that Jim East was sheriff in a total area that equalled Connecticut, Rhode Island, and Delaware combined.

That was the situation Shaw Buckner faced; he was the sole officer of the law from the Wyoming border to the north reaches of the Missouri River, which was a goodly piece of real estate, even to someone used to thinking Texas-big.

And Simon Boxley was sadly mistaken in his belief that Shaw Buckner had no right to arrest him.

Judge Little was like his name, a wisp of a man, frail to the point of delicacy, with a disorderly shock of hair and fearless eyes. He brought the hearing to order without banging his gavel or raising his voice and the clerk read the indictments as prepared by the county attorney.

"Let me say," Little began, "that this is not a trial. It is a hearing to determine whether or not the charges are true and just. If they are, the accused persons will be held in custody and bound over for trial. If the charges are unfounded, the principals will be released. Is the attorney for the people ready?"

The county attorney stood up. "Yes, Your Honor."

Little looked to the other table. "Defense?"

"Yes, Your Honor."

Little nodded. "I have before me a motion submitted by Mr. McCall requesting that—The Dingo Kid?" He flicked his glance up and the Association lawyer stood up.

"That's right, Your Honor."

"Most unusual name." He read on. "—and Dandy McGee be tried separately. I'm ready to hear argument, Counselor."

McCall took off his glasses and pocketed them. "Your Honor, Dandy McGee and The Dingo Kid are both employed by Mr. O. B. Hardison and have proved to be reliable, trustworthy, and in general, top hands. Mr. Hardison—as well as myself—feels strongly that both these men were acting within the framework of brand interest when they engaged in this rustling venture for the sole purpose of exposing the outlaws and bringing them to justice. With your honor's permission, I would like to call my first witness to substantiate this premise."

Little nodded and the clerk said, "Mr. Buster

Mills, takethestandplease." I did and he administered the oath. "Doyousolemnlypromise-totellthetruththewholetruthandnothingbutthetruth-sohelpyouGod?"

"Yes, I do." I sat down and waited for McCall to speak. He put on his glasses.

We went all through the business of establishing my relationship with The Dingo Kid and Dandy McGee, and my position with the brand, then we got into the actual business of the rustlers. I told the court how Hardpan and Oily Swede had approached me, and what I had done about it.

Little listened carefully and McCall paced about a bit. "Now, Buster, let's establish a few facts. We've already determined that you know a good bit about beef work, as you put it. Can you tell me why the rustlers would take only the calves?"

"They hadn't been branded yet," I said. "How a rustler works always depends on his market, how close it is, and how quickly he can get rid of the rustled stock. If a man had a slaughter yard close by that wasn't fussy, he could rustle a branded steer. But if he has to hold stock, or throw the calves in with his own herd, or drive them a good piece, he wouldn't dare rustle branded stock. A drying hide in the tack shed will get a man hung if it has the wrong brand on it. Maybe quicker because if a man's altered the brand, the scar from the old one will show clearly on the underside of the hide."

McCall nodded. "So the rustlers were forced to steal unbranded calves?"

"Yes."

"I see. Then the rustlers, forced to steal unbranded stock, had to do one or two things with them. They had to add them to their own herd or sell them at some market place."

"That's right."

"But these men were driving toward a market in the mining country. Can you tell the court why?"

"They didn't have any choice. Boxley couldn't add that many to his own herd without arousing suspicion. And none of the others had a registered brand." I smiled. "People get suspicious of ranchers who have cows that drop two calves a year. But the important thing to remember is that a rustler rustles to make money. To do that you have to market the beef, not add them to your herd."

"Thank you," McCall said and polished his glasses. "Buster, do you believe that The Dingo Kid and Dandy McGee participated in the rustling activity for the sole purpose of capturing the whole gang?"

"Yes, sir."

"Why do you say that?"

"They had no reason to rustle Broken T stock. Their cut of the profits of the rustled herd wouldn't have amounted to enough to make it worth their while, and you can't forget that a man rustles for money, not for the fun of it. Add to that the fact that they just couldn't get away with it because they'd be missed by other than the crew they were working with. And Dandy McGee came back and told us all about it. Now no man is going to stick his neck in a noose just for the fun of it."

"Thank you, Buster," McCall said, and smiled. "Your witness."

Boxley's attorney was from Bozeman. He was a pleasant, deliberate man who smiled as he approached. "Buster, my name is Howard Frank. I'd like to ask you a few questions. Isn't it a fact that both Dandy McGee and The Dingo Kid are wanted in Arizona for stage holdups?"

"Yes."

"Yet you want us to believe that these confirmed outlaws are above cattle rustling?" He laughed at the whole idea and patted his mustache. "Let's take up another point. When Hardpan and this other man, Oily Swede, came to you, they believed that Dandy and Dingo were rustling, didn't they?"

"Yes, they thought that."

"Well, then if these men, who have known them longer than you have believed they were rustling, isn't it a little far-fetched to accept your judgment?" He rocked back on his heels. "I suggest, Buster, that Dandy and Dingo fully intended to enter into the rustling venture, and then when they saw that there was no profit in it, they decided to betray the men who had put trust in them and claim the reward." He wheeled about. "I have no further questions to put to this witness."

I was told to step down and I took a seat in the spectator section and Charlie Hatch took the stand. He covered nearly the same ground as I did and then Howard Frank had his turn to carve him into little pieces. Only while I had been easy, Charlie Hatch was not.

Frank made his first mistake by calling Charlie by his first name and when the hassle died down, Frank was instructed by the judge to cease these familiarities and address the witness as Mr. Hatch.

A smart man would have realized that in putting a brand on Charlie Hatch you were just bound to get mauled a bit, but Frank had his points to make and enough stubbornness to forge on. "Mr. Hatch, you are of course completely familiar with the lawless background of Dandy McGee and The Dingo Kid, so let us go on to more germane issues."

"All right, let's go," Charlie said and crossed his legs.

Frowning, Howard Frank said, "It is not necessary to re-enforce my statements."

Charlie seemed surprised. "You said let's go on and I said all right let's go and I don't see anything wrong with that." He looked around the courtroom as though trying to find any man so dense he didn't find sense in that.

Howard Frank turned to the judge as though to appeal, then thought better of it and returned his attention to the witness. "Mr. Hatch, since you are directly responsible for a large portion of Broken T, I want your reaction to the news Dandy McGee brought."

"I thought it was the greatest thing since matches," Charlie Hatch said.

"You believed him?"

"Certainly. He had no love for Simon Boxley. Fact is, he hauled off once and hit him in the mouth. Dandy would have bedded down with a rattlesnake before he'd throw in with the Boxley crowd."

Frank laughed. "Really, now do you expect the court to believe that Simon Boxley was unaware of this and would accept him?"

"You're claiming that he did and that Dandy and Dingo were part of the rustlers. Remember, I'm the one who's saying they're not."

"Don't twist my words!" He calmed himself and went on. "What I mean—and you well know it— was that Simon Boxley would be a fool to trust Dandy McGee, a known enemy."

"Boxley's a fool all right," Charlie said.

"I'm not interested in your opinion!"

"Suit yourself," Charlie Hatch said, "but when you put him on the stand you're going to find he ain't any too bright." He chuckled and drew Judge Little's frown.

"I have no further questions," Frank said and Charlie went to the spectator's seats and took one.

McCall made a summation to Judge Little and it was a nice piece of oratory, to the point, and clearly pointing out the factors that led Dandy McGee and The Dingo Kid to go ahead with their participation in the rustling venture without first notifying Charlie Hatch of their intentions. First, Charlie was not readily available, and second they had to move immediately or not at all. He presented a good argument, logical in every way and I thought that the judge was impressed.

Howard Frank was pretty noisy by comparison and he did his best to link Dandy and Dingo into the rustling activity. I thought this was strange, his virtually admitting that Simon Boxley was a rustler, then I realized that this was an issue divorced from the argument at hand and for his own purposes Frank could admit that Boxley was a rustler and then during the actual trial, reverse himself and plead complete innocence.

Judge Little adjourned until two o'clock to give himself time to consider the case and Charlie Hatch and I went to the hotel and had our noon meal with Tess O'Shanessy. We didn't talk about the hearing; there wasn't any sense to it and speculation was just that, a worry and completely useless. The whole thing was in Judge Little's hands and his judgment would determine whether or not Dandy McGee and The Dingo Kid stood trial for rustling or went free.

Tess O'Shanessy said, "Dingo came into the store this morning and I think he's more worried about getting the reward money than being hung."

"We're not goin' to talk about it," Charlie said.

"All right, you're not, but I am. Sad-eye's wife is sure showing her condition. And every day Sad-eye gets more confused, trying to figure out which is best, being happy over the coming event, or worrying himself sick over it."

"It's hell when people don't have enough money," Charlie Hatch said. He ate some of his roast beef and then pushed the plate aside before he was half through. "When are they going to get a decent cook in this place?"

"Crabcrabcrab," Tess said, and frowned when he frowned. "You never say that about my meals."

"That's 'cause I don't look good with a fat lip," Charlie admitted.

"Tell me that I cook well."

"You cook real well."

"Am I pretty?"

"Pretty too," he said, and glanced at me. "You eat slow, Buster."

"Why, I was just watching you get backed into that corner," I said. "Enjoying it too."

"Some men like to see others suffer," Charlie said.

"You're not suffering," I said, and got up from the table. "I'll play the banjo at your wedding."

"What wedding?" Charlie Hatch asked.

I smiled and mussed his hair, rocking his head back and forth the way he always rocked mine. "Friend, no one is *that* dumb."

Going back to the courthouse, I found The Dingo Kid and Dandy McGee holding down the steps and I sat with them, sharing their tobacco. "Now there's no need to look so worried," I told them.

"I always get worried when a judge is fooling around with me," Dandy said.

"Bein' married is hell," Dingo said. "Well, look at how much it costs. You've got to have a house and furniture, and there's sure to be kids. A man don't have one damned dime to call his own. Hell, it's cheaper to buy it."

"A man falls in love once in awhile," I said. "He can't help himself. Can't go against nature."

"Yeah," Dingo admitted, "that's sure as hell so. Caught myself just in time a couple of times. When I find myself gettin' interested in a woman I get on my horse and make tracks."

Shaw Buckner came out and said, "Judge is entering his chambers. Come inside if you want."

We got up and went in and took seats. A few minutes later Charlie and the lawyers showed up and we stood while the judge seated himself then waited.

"Gentlemen, I've given the evidence and arguments due consideration and I see no call to try The Dingo Kid and Dandy McGee separately from the others. However, I would like to advise the county prosecutor that his evidence against these two men is flimsy at best and I seriously doubt that a jury would convict. If the case were being tried before me I would dismiss it because they were both instrumental in the capture of the rustlers and the herd. The bench would entertain a motion from the county prosecutor to dismiss the charges."

"I so move, your honor."

"The clerk will record that," Little said. "Now there is the matter of the reward offered by the Cattlemen's Association which they have left to me to adjudicate. Since the actual involvement of Dandy McGee and The Dingo Kid is subjective and purely a matter of personal perspective, and since no formal charges have been made, it is the court's ruling that the reward money be evenly divided between Charlie Hatch, Buster Mills, the man called Hardpan, and Oily Swede." He looked up. "Don't you gentlemen believe in given names? No matter. The sum of five hundred dollars will be divided and the clerk will pay that amount. The prisoners will remain in the custody of the sheriff and trial will be set in ten days. Dismissed."

Dingo and Dandy hurried out and I wanted to

follow them but there was that business of collecting the money and signing for it and by the time I got out of there they were gone.

For an hour I combed the streets, going in one saloon after another, and finally I got to the stable. The hostler was there and he said that they had got their horses and left town, taking the south road.

In a way I was relieved because they were probably heading for Moon Creek. It was just as well because they would be discouraged and down at the mouth and if they remained in town they'd both get drunk and get into a fight and spend a couple of days in Buckner's jail.

While I had been chasing Dingo and Dandy, Hardpan and Oily Swede had been looking for me.

"Want to talk to you, Buster," Hardpan said. They flanked me and we walked slowly back toward the center of town. "We've been thinkin' that it was a shame Dandy and Dingo got gypped out of the money because we know what they intended to do with it."

"Well, they didn't count on it turning out the way it did," I said.

"We kind of thought that if you liked the idea, we'd pool the money and do what they planned. You know, give it to the doc to pay for Sad-eye's wife."

I had good use for that money; it was a windfall to me, and I hadn't really thought of giving it away, but Hardpan was right, this was the right thing to do. "All right. Have you talked to Charlie Hatch yet?"

"Would you do that for us?"

"Why me always?" Then I laughed. "All right. You want to give me the money now?"

They dug into their pockets for it and gave it to me. Then Hardpan smiled. "I guess Swede and I'll go on out to the ranch. It's all right if we tell Dingo? They'll feel better."

"Go ahead and tell him," I said and went on toward O'Shanessy's store. Charlie Hatch was there, just as I guessed he'd be. I laid the money on the counter and said, "Oily Swede and Hardpan gave me this to give to Doc Springer. I'm putting in my share, Charlie."

"A hundred and twenty-five dollars? Buster, that's more than enough to move your family up here."

"Yes, but I'll just have to do it some other way, Charlie."

"Buster, all three of you are damned fools. That money is yours, free and clear."

"Sure is," I said. Tess was watching him carefully; she glanced at me, then looked again at Charlie Hatch. "But I've got to live with myself, Charlie. Suppose anything happened to Sad-eye's wife? How much enjoyment would I get out of the money then? I just can't buy what I want at the expense of someone else. Dingo and Dandy took their chances and the judge could have said to hell with you and made them stand trial." I shook my head. "My share goes to the doc. How about you?"

"You swore," Tess said.

"I did?"

"You said hell."

"Never mind that," I said. "What about it, Charlie?"

"I don't have it," he told me, shrugging.

"Where the hell is it?"

"That's twice," Tess said.

I ignored her. "You goin' to tell me, Charlie?"

"Sure," he said. "I already took mine over to the doc's."

I blew out a long breath. "Then what's the idea of ragging me?"

"Didn't hurt you any, did it?" He laughed. "I already told Doc you'd be over with yours."

"Now that's a fine howdydo!"

"Well, that's what you decided, wasn't it?"

"I like a chance to make up my mind, that's all." Then I smiled and let it build into a chuckle. "Charlie, you're a son of a gun, that's what you are."

"Now that's what you say because Tess is here. It'd be somethin' else if she wasn't."

"I can leave," she said.

"Never mind," I told her. "I'm going over to the doc's house."

"All right," Charlie said. "You goin' back to Moon Creek tonight?"

It was a question, a simple one, but what he was really saying was that I was done being a school teacher and now that the hearing was over I had to get back to my job.

"Yes, I'll be out of town in an hour. Unless Shaw Buckner wants me to stay."

"There's no reason for that," Charlie said.

Tess stepped past him. "Buster, thank you for what you did for the children. The parents will want to thank you too."

"It wasn't anything," I said and got out of there because it was something and I didn't want Tess or Charlie to see how much it really was.

The regular teacher would be coming back in a month so I didn't see any sense in making a lot of talk over it. There was no sense in clinging to something that wouldn't last or come to anything anyway.

Doctor Springer was in his office, reading; he put the book down when I came in. I gave him the money and he put it into a metal cash box. Then he took off his glasses and wiped them and said, "Buster, this is as fine a thing as any man can do for another."

"It's what Dingo and Dandy wanted."

"Yes, I heard about it. And when I see Sad-eye Nolan again I'm going to take a good careful look

175

at him to see what kind of a man he really is to deserve such friends."

"Sad-eye's all right."

Springer nodded and flicked his eyebrows up. "Are you through with the school now, Buster?"

"All done. Back to beef work."

"What a damned waste. You had my boy. Failing in reading. Now he wants to read. That's something, Buster, giving a boy the incentive to want to do something."

"Well, it was somebody new," I said. "That makes the difference I guess."

He looked at me and saw that I didn't want to talk about it. "Thank you just the same, Buster. I'll see that this money is taken to the right place."

After I left his office I was in a hurry to get out of town and move back into the bunkhouse and the routine of ranch work. It was as though I was leaving too much behind and distance would help. Distance and dawn-to-dark work.

11.

ON THE way to Moon Creek I met Sad-eye Nolan with a string of wagons; he pulled his to one side and sent the others on and when the dust cleared we exchanged tobacco and smoked. Sad-eye allowed that he was getting along tolerably well and he liked town living and family life although his wife's condition was getting a little delicate.

176

"She sure does want this baby," Sad-eye said, shaking his head. "Me too, but it means somethin' special to her. Her other husband couldn't have kids, I guess, and it was a disappointment to her, though she probably never ragged him about it. Wasn't her way, you know. She's easy to get along with."

"When are you going to move to Billings?"

He shrugged. "Next month sometime. Don't know how I can afford it though. Can't afford not to either."

"These things have a way of working out, Sad-eye."

"You got faith, Buster. Maybe I'll get it someday. Been a loner all my life. Changin' takes time." He drew on his smoke then pinched it out. "Pretty excitin' news, catchin' those rustlers. Seems like some people have all the fun."

"You've got to live right, Sad-eye."

"Tryin'," he said. "Lord knows I'm tryin'. Cut out drinkin' and cards. Don't hardly chaw no more either. You might say that I've been divested of my sins. And since I take care not to cuss around the house, I've learned to live without that, too." He smiled. "You could say that when a man stops sayin' horseshit to everything he's finally becomin' civilized." He lifted the reins. "Well, I've got to go or get too far behind. See you, Buster."

We went our own ways.

Bullmoose Reilly was in charge of Moon Creek until Charlie Hatch returned and he sent me south along the Tongue to join a branding crew working that section of the county, which was all right with me. It was a day and a half ride and I got there in the young afternoon and went right to work. They had two good men tending the irons and fire and three branding so I shook out my catch rope and helped keep them busy.

This is hot, dusty work and when it is done each day a man is ready to go sit in the handiest creek just for the sheer pleasure of it. We moved four times in two weeks and it would be another twenty days before we were through.

Charlie Hatch rode in one day and pulled part of the crew off to go haying with the farmers. I didn't get a chance to talk to him until that evening and he said that Sad-eye Nolan had taken his wife to Billings and wouldn't be back until after the baby was born.

"Sad-eye like to worried himself sick over the money," Charlie said. "Finally Doc Springer had to tell him where it came from and old Sad-eye just busted down and bawled. It was a very touchin' thing, I can tell you."

"It's nice that he can stop worrying," I said.

"He'll find somethin' else to worry about."

"Did Simon Boxley have his trial yet?"

"Oh, sure."

"Well, don't just say 'oh sure.' I was there, Charlie,

and I want to know what the devil happened."

He smiled, stringing me along. "They're goin' to hang old Simon come winter. His lawyer's fixin' to appeal so they're goin' to give him enough time to have it turned down."

"What about his boys and the others?"

"Jail. Four years. The county is tryin' now to find where they can send 'em. Shaw's afraid he'll have to keep 'em that long. Meals come out of his pocket, you know." He chuckled at the idea of it.

"I've been expecting to be called as a witness," I said.

"Wasn't any need. Boxley pleaded guilty and threw himself on the mercy of the court. Well, he'll get a quick drop. That's merciful enough."

"Hanging is a bad thing."

"So is stealing a man's cattle," Charlie Hatch said and felt quite righteous about it, and in his way he was right. Cattle was his bed and board, his life, his work, and he would fight for land or stock on the land. I felt the same way only I would have driven Boxley out of the country, but Charlie Hatch didn't believe in that.

Mine was definitely a minority view.

"I read in the Billings paper that some of our territorial representatives are in Washington, trying to get statehood for Montana."

"What does O. B. Hardison think of that?" I asked.

"He's for it," Charlie said, smiling. "Why not? He owns nearly all the land and what he don't own outright is being homesteaded now. You want to homestead some for the old man? He'll pay you five hundred dollars for your section when you prove up."

I shook my head. "If I put five years into a place I'd keep it."

"It ain't that hard. All you need is a shack with one door and one window and—"

"It's not for me," I told him.

"Well, I didn't think it was. Anyway, I want you to come back to Moon Creek in the morning. Got a small herd that has to be driven to Crow Rock. You can take Hardpan and Oily Swede along. Pick two others, whoever you like." He got up and stretched.

"Who's heading this up?"

"You are," he said, and went to get his horse.

That night, after supper, I cut out a good horse, saddled, lashed on my roll and rode north to Moon Creek and got there late. There were plenty of empty bunks to roll into and in the morning the cook woke me by beating an old branding iron against a wagon rim. There were about twenty hands at Moon Creek, most of them coming and going and I asked about The Dingo Kid and Dandy McGee, but no one had seen them for a spell, which wasn't odd because the ranch was so large and the crews were scattered to the four corners of it.

Hardpan and Oily Swede were waiting for me, so I picked one more man, a colored cowboy called Inky Potter; he was a man of fifty who had been working beef all his life and he was reliable. Since our herd was small, about seventy head, we decided to get going; the four of us could handle it all right, and Charlie Hatch agreed because he had a delivery date promised and was pushed for time.

Many of the small ranchers bought heifers from Broken T because they couldn't afford a blooded bull and improving their stock was quite a problem unless they bought good heifers to breed. And no one who intended staying in the cattle business could survive without going to the Hereford strain.

Charlie Hatch gave me a bill of sale signed by him; when I delivered the cattle to Candless I'd get the money, then sign the bill of sale and turn it over to him. In two weeks I'd be back at the home place.

No trouble at all.

We left the Moon Creek place, moving the herd easily because we didn't want to walk them gaunt. Ten miles a day was an easy pace and in a week we came onto Candless' land; he had a place in the northeast corner of Rosebud County, a couple of sections with a good log house and a stout barn and corral. Candless and his wife had two nearly-grown sons and they worked the place without additional hands, so after delivering the herd, we rode into Crow Rock. The banker would pay me for the cattle and I'd turn the bill of sale over to him.

This meant a night in town, a few drinks, some sitting around and then the ride back to Moon Creek. And that doesn't sound like much but to men who work from dawn to dark seven days a week it is a lot.

We tied up in front of Grizby's and they went in while I walked a half block down to the bank, which was little more than a log building with a big safe sitting toward the back of the room. The banker was alone and we transacted our business in a matter of minutes; I imagine he was loaning the money to Candless but since it was none of my business I didn't inquire.

"Mighty upsetting," the banker said, "this rustling business. Many of us disliked Boxley but we had to get along with him. However, it's worked out for the best. Ardy Potter came in and picked up Boxley's outstanding notes and has moved onto what was Leaning S land. It'll be another year before it gets straightened out as to how much Potter acquired, but he's a good man, honest, and not riding over everyone all the time."

"Boxley didn't have any other kin then?"

The banker shrugged. "A wife and a couple of cousins but they packed up and went back to

Texas at the first smell of trouble. Took what was on their backs and what they could get on a horse."

"Well, maybe Broken T did you a favor," I said.

"It looks that way. Been an exciting summer. About ten days ago the Billings stage was robbed."

"I never heard about that."

"Fact, and it was something all right. The shotgun guard tried to draw his pistol and was shot. He's recovering, but I hear it was a close one. A lot of shooting."

"Did the bandits—"

"Didn't get a dime, Buster. The horses bolted and the driver didn't get them whoaed until he was a mile down the road." He laughed. "We never saw anything of the bandits."

"You were lucky," I said, and went down to Grizby's store. The others were leaning against the bar with their beer and I ordered and began to kill time.

Esther came from the back, glanced at us, and recognized me. She said, "Did you bring your banjo, Buster?"

I shook my head. "Not much time for playing. I'm heading back in the morning."

"Papa bought an old spinet organ for me. Would you like to see it?"

I frowned, wondering why, then shrugged and turned into the back with her; they had quarters there, three rooms and a kitchen and she looked back to make sure she wouldn't be overheard.

"You've got to help me," she said softly. "The one called Dandy is hiding out here. He's hurt and he won't let me fetch the doctor."

"Dandy here? Hurt?" Then I made a guess. "He was one of the bandits."

"He's been shot. I've been hiding him in a shack down the street."

"What about The Dingo Kid?"

"He was here, but he left yesterday." She looked at me pleadingly. "Help me. Please?"

"Sure I will," I said. "When can I go to him?"

"It'll be dark soon. Wait for me out back in the alley."

Then I went back to the bar and picked up what was left of my beer and fell into a deep silence. Those two damned fools were trying to get money for Sad-eye Nolan, not knowing that it had already been taken care of. Finally I made up my mind what I was going to do and I drew them over to a table for a sit down and some quiet talk. I told them about the holdup attempt and that Esther had been hiding Dandy and taking care of him.

"Now we sure as hell can't let him die or get hung," I said. And they all agreed to that. "As soon as it gets dark we'll get him out of town, make camp, and then send for the doctor. We'll tell him that Dandy was with us all along and that he had an accident, his gun fell out of the holster while he was riding and went off. Everybody got that straight?"

They murmured and nodded.

"Where's Dingo?" Hardpan asked.

"Unless I miss my guess, he's out trying to pull another holdup seeing as how he got nothing off the stage." A bit of a notion was coming to me and I said, "Hardpan, as soon as we get Dandy taken care of, make a travois and start back. I'm going on to Billings."

"That's a good four days' ride from here," Hardpan said.

"Yes, and Dingo's got a one day head start already. But I figure it'll take him a day or two to find a henhouse to break into and I might be able to stop him."

"What'll I tell Charlie?" Hardpan asked.

"The truth," I said.

It seemed a long time getting dark and finally I left and went around in back and soon Esther came out. She took my hand and we walked down the dark, littered alley to an old shed. She used a side door and once inside she groped for a ladder to the loft and went up first.

I heard a pistol being cocked and said, "It's me, Buster."

Dandy McGee sighed with relief and put his gun down. I moved to his bed of hay and old blankets. "Where are you hit?"

"Thigh," he said. "Can't walk."

"The bullet still in there?"

"No," he said, "I dug it out with my knife three days ago."

Esther put a match to a candle and I saw that there were blankets hung over the window so that no light passed through. Dandy McGee's leg was bandaged and his eyes were gaunt, as though he had been running a fever.

"I've put carbolic salve on his leg," Esther said. "It was all I had but there ain't much pus."

"We'll get you to a doctor," I said. "Hardpan and Oily Swede will be here soon and we'll get you out of here."

"And how do you explain this bullet hole?"

"We'll lie for you," I said. "Dandy, you blasted fool, Sad-eye already had the money. All of us chipped in and gave him the reward money only you didn't stick around long enough to find that out."

He looked at me stupidly, then swore softly, and shook his head. "I guess we both should have known. Now ain't that a joke on us?"

"A hell of a joke if I don't catch up with Dingo before he goes and does something else stupid," I said. "Did he go to Billings?"

"Yeah. He figured he'd find something there he could stick up."

The door opened downstairs and Esther went to see who it was, then Hardpan and the others came up the ladder.

"Ain't you a pretty one," Hardpan said, clucking. "Well, let's get him out of here."

"Where's Inky Potter?" I asked.

"Huntin' the doc," Hardpan said. "We've made camp just past the edge of town. Come on, Oily, bear a hand and lift easy. He looks a little peeked."

They handed him down the ladder, being as gentle as possible and I hung back with Esther while she blew out the candle. Then we went down and Hardpan and Oily Swede were already carrying Dandy McGee down the dark alley.

"Will he be all right now?" she asked.

"We'll see to him, Esther. You've done a nice thing for him."

"He came to me," she said, speaking very softly. "Late at night he came to my window and tapped and I went out and found him in the alley where he'd fallen."

Suddenly a lot of things fell into place for me and I said, "Esther, do you want to go with him?"

"Yes." Then she touched me lightly. "But do you think he wants me?"

"He came to you, didn't he?"

"That's so. But I'm not pretty, Buster."

"I don't think he thought of that at all. Do you want me to talk to your father?"

"What would you say?"

"I guess that you loved Dandy McGee and wanted to be with him. What else is there?"

"He wouldn't understand that."

"Does he have much choice? Come on, I'll walk you back." When we reached the rear door I let her go in, then said, "I'm going out to the camp but I'll be back."

"Ask him if he wants me, Buster."

"All right," I said, and walked around to the front street. Inky Potter and the doctor were hurrying by and I let them go on and followed a moment later, arriving when the doctor was making his examination. He and Hardpan were talking and the doctor was in a fretful mood.

"You should have seen a doctor three or four days ago!"

"Warn't none," Hardpan insisted.

The doctor looked around when I stepped up to the fire. "Are you in charge here?"

"Yes."

"Why wasn't this man given medical treatment?"

I shrugged. "Well, it was only in the thigh and there were no doctors between here and Miles City."

The doctor swore, including all of us with that single word. He cleaned the wound, applied a disinfectant and a heavy bandage. "I suppose you doctored this yourself?"

"Yep," Hardpan said, smiling. "Good job, huh?"

"Atrocious!"

Hardpan looked at me. "Does that mean good?"

"It means you don't know your ass from a warm

rock!" the doctor snapped. "How long have you been in town anyway?"

"Oh, five hours," I said.

"And you just called me?" He sounded as though he couldn't believe this.

"Well," Hardpan told him, "we didn't want to kick up a fuss about this. After all, he dropped his own gun and it went off; it wasn't any of our doin'."

"We're leaving in the morning," I put in, "and I thought it would be nice if a doctor looked at him. Then if he dies he can't say we didn't do our best."

The doctor became so angry that he sputtered and couldn't talk. Finally he calmed himself. "Believe me, never in my life have I seen such heartless, cold-blooded, thoughtless people." He gave me some salve and bandages and a pint bottle of medicine. "This is a solution that will keep the infection down and promote healing, and the bandages are to be used on his leg, not for any selfish purpose you might think of. The salve will keep the wound moist. Oh, it'll heal but it'll leave a very bad scar, thanks to your stupid neglect."

"That sure is nice of you, doc," Hardpan said, ingratiatingly.

"My fee is three dollars. If any of you have that much."

I paid him and he turned and went back toward town. Then he thought of something and came back. "I would suggest that you do not put this man astraddle a horse and make him ride back. He is weak from loss of blood and fever and he'll surely die if you make him sit a saddle, although I don't suppose his dying would sadden any of you at all. Make one of those Indian things and pull him behind a horse. And pull him slowly, understand? Very slowly."

"We'll take your advice, doc," I said. "And for a greenhorn you're a real gentleman."

"The hell with that," he said, and walked away and we had to hold ourselves in to keep from laughing.

When he was well out of earshot, Inky Potter said, "We sho did foo' dat man."

"Yes, he's so mad at us that he never once doubted that we were telling the truth." I looked at Dandy McGee. "I don't know whether to cuss you or what. You've been a jackass, Dandy. Three kinds of a jackass."

"I've been mighty foolish all right. But I don't blame Dingo. He wanted to go it alone but I wouldn't let him." He sighed and rubbed his hands across his chest and pulled the blanket up to his chin. "That damned shotgun guard threw down on us with his pistol. Dingo shot a couple of times and missed him and then the guard shot me and I shot back." He shook his head slowly. "I sure didn't mean to kill him. God knows I didn't."

"He's not dead," I said. "I ought to have kept

that to myself and made you sweat over it, but I'm just not that mean." I waved to the others. "Go see to the horses or something while Dandy and I have a talk."

After they walked away I squatted by Dandy and said, "I hope you don't think you're going to get away with this. Candless knows you didn't come up with us and when he hears about this he'll put two and two together and get the right answer. And the doctor will get over his huff and figure it out. He'll remember how the wound looked and know that you couldn't have gotten it the way we said. But we'll be gone by then, Dandy, and you can breathe easy."

"What are you tryin' to rub my nose in, Buster?"

"This is the end of it, Dandy. No more half-retired stage bandit. You give me your solemn word you're through or I'll take you back and turn you over to Shaw Buckner."

"Would you really do that?"

"Try me."

He studied me a moment, then shook his head. "No, you'd do it."

"Tell me something else. How come you went to Esther?"

He thought about it. "I remembered her from the last time we were here, Buster, the way she was and I knew she'd help me. There wasn't anyone else I could turn to."

"She's homely," I said. "Her nose is too big and

191

her eyes are too close together. Time she's thirty she'll have grown a mustache."

"That's a goddamned—!" he yelled and then fell silent for a moment. I waited for him to say something else. "Why am I wrong so much of the time, Buster? I remember what I said to Charlie about her bein' homely and a dozen times now I wish I could take it back."

"Why do you think she helped you, Dandy? Because she's good?" He started to look away from me but I put my hand around his chin and turned his face back. "She wanted me to ask you something. She wants to know if she can go with you. Isn't that something, Dandy? She'll be satisfied just to be in love with you. It doesn't matter if you love her or not, as long as she can go with you."

"She shouldn't talk like that," McGee said quickly. "It's not right. Well, what does a man like me say, Buster?"

"I want you to talk to her, Dandy. I'll go to town and fetch her for you."

"Don't do that! Buster, let it go this way; it'll be better for her."

"Then you want me to tell her that you don't want her?"

He shook his head.

"Seems to me you ought to make up your mind, Dandy."

"She's too good to take and live with and I ain't

good enough for her to marry." He shook his head again. "You go see her and tell her that if things work out all right I'll send for her. Tell her that when that time comes I'll have a home for her. Will you do that, Buster?"

"Sure, I'll tell her anything you say."

Dandy McGee grinned. "I'm glad I got shot. Yes, I really am. It stopped me, Buster. It made me think for once." He reached out and gripped my wrist. "Are you going to stop Dingo?"

"If I can. If it's not too late."

12

GOING TO Billings wasn't just a matter of getting on my horse and leaving; I had responsibilities to the brand that I couldn't just push aside. I found where the express agent lived and got him to put the money in his safe and consigned it to Charlie Hatch at the Miles City office.

Then I found the telegrapher and composed a message to Charlie Hatch in which I advised him that Dingo was going to do something foolish in the line of his former work and that I was going to Billings to see if I could stop him. I also explained that Dandy would be coming back with Hardpan and the others and that he would explain in detail just how and why they had gotten into trouble.

Grizby's was my last stop; the place was nearly deserted and he was cleaning up a little. Esther was in the kitchen and I went on back and left the connecting door open in case Grizby got any funny notions in his head. She was at the wooden sink, cleaning the last of the pots and pans and she turned when she heard my step.

"He didn't want me," she said, as though it was no surprise to her.

"I guess the truth of it is that he wants you too much to have you go like this, running off with him. He's goin' to send for you, Esther."

"No, he'll forget about me."

"You're a fool if you think that," I said, bluntly. "I've got to leave town now. Stayed too long already. But I tell you what. You go to him tonight. We're camped right out to the edge of town. You go to him once more, talk to him, then make up your mind whether or not he means it. Will you do that?"

"It's bad enough just havin' him go."

"Well, then you stay here and feel sorry for yourself," I snapped. "Goodbye, Esther."

I left the kitchen. Grizby was behind the counter and he stopped me with a nod. "Couldn't help overhearin'. Been some worry to me, Buster, her runnin' off with the first man that smiled. Guess there's more to Dandy than I thought."

"You knew he was in town?" Grizby nodded.

"She never could fool me, Buster. Knew she took grub to him and sneaked out late after I went to bed." He sighed. "I want her to have a good

194

man, Buster." He tapped himself on the chest. "There's a lot to that girl. A lot that don't show at first look."

"He knows that."

"I guess. Got everythin' you need?" He put a sack on the counter. "Some canned things in there. Good luck."

I nodded and took the sack and went out to get my horse. The street was deserted when I left town and I didn't bother to stop at our camp because I'd already frittered away too much time and The Dingo Kid had a head start on me that I couldn't hope to make up.

Billings lay to the southwest and although my desire was to ride in that direction I deliberately held pretty much to a southerly course, hoping to meet the Miles City–Billings stage road before it forked and got me hopelessly lost. I didn't know the country and I wouldn't recognize the Billings road if I stumbled across it so it was important that I get on it early, before it forked and that way I'd know whether or not I was on the right one.

I wore out the night and the horse in the hills and come dawn I broke over a ridge and saw a cabin off to the left in a kidney-shaped valley. So I cut toward it, making enough racket as I drummed across the flats to set the dog barking. A man came out with a repeating rifle and some caution in his eyes, then he saw the brand on my horse and put the rifle down.

"You ride like a man with a place to go and not much time to get there," he said. "Got time to light for coffee and grits?"

"Yes, if you can give me a fresh horse," I said. He nodded and I stripped off saddle and roll and rifle and dropped them by his door then turned the horse into the corral before washing up. The man had a wife and three boys, two of them in their teens and the youngest just old enough to talk a lot.

"Don't see much of Broken T around here 'cept at roundup," the man said. "Name's Bailey. Ed Bailey. This is my wife, Rose. Sit. We was about to."

A plate was put before me, scrapple and ham and plenty of coffee. My hunger was a gnawing in my stomach and I ate awhile before I started to talk. "Mr. Bailey, could you tell me where I am in relation to the Billings road?"

"You be at the west end of the Scottie Creek," Bailey said. He turned in his chair and pointed out the open door at the mountains. "You continue on the direction you been headin' and by nightfall you ought to come to the road. Cross it 'cause you're above the fork. Shortly after you'll have to ford the Yellowstone. Reckon you can make it this time of the year if you're a strong swimmer. A bit later you'll come to another road that'll take you on into Billings." He looked at me carefully and noticed the pistol in the holster sewed to my chap leg. "Was I you I'd stay awake along that road. You ain't so far from the Crow reservation and now and then a few of the bucks get the notion they ought to ride around and raise hell."

"I'll take care," I said, and finished my breakfast. Bailey went outside with me while I caught up one of his horses and saddled. We shook hands and I said, "Appreciate the meal. You'll get your horse back."

"Don't worry me none. Don't let it worry you either." He smiled and waved and I rode out of the yard, heading for the high slot in the mountains that he had indicated.

Came noon and the horse was tiring badly and so was I; after tying him I stretched out on the ground and slept for three hours and woke stiff and bleary-eyed. It bothered me to have wasted the time but I knew that I'd do better with rest and the horse had to be saved; if I wore him out before we reached the river he'd be too tired to swim and that river was always swift and dangerous.

Like Bailey had said, come evening I hit the road, crossed it, and just before dark I reached the river and spent a few minutes looking it over. The water was roiling and breaking over the boulders in the river bed; it wasn't very wide but it was going to be a tough swim.

I took off my chaps and boots and tied them to the saddle and shed my brush jacket and stuffed it into my blanket roll, then mounted and urged the horse into the water. He didn't want to but I gave him no choice and as soon as he went swimming deep I left the saddle and let him strike out by himself, and just hung onto his tail and kicked.

The current took us like a couple of corks in a swirled washtub and swept us downstream and I didn't even try to fight this; my interest was concentrated on that other shore and when we reached it I just didn't turn loose of the horse and let him run off. I caught a stirrup and dug in both feet and swung him around until I could grab the reins.

Then I tied him to some heavy brush and went along the bank and gathered wood and got dry matches out of my jumper pocket and built a roaring fire. When I toasted myself dry I put on my boots and chaps, ate, fed the horse, then mounted up although I was ready to fall out of the saddle any time.

I wanted to reach that road even though it was growing rapidly dark so I pushed on and finally came to it; it wasn't but a mile or so although it seemed like five. There I built another fire, picketed the horse and rolled into my blankets.

How long I slept I wasn't sure but when I woke it was cold and it seemed as though dawn wasn't far off. I heard a sound, the jangle of harness and the crunch of wheels on the pebbles in the road and I knew that this was what had brought me awake. Quickly I fed brush to the fire and got it going, then the stage pulled into view and hauled up.

The shotgun guard said, "Make a move, friend, and it'll be your last."

"This isn't a holdup," I said but still kept both hands in plain sight.

Then Charlie Hatch stuck his head out and said, "It's all right, Spotty. That's Buster Mills."

To find Charlie aboard the stage was a big surprise; he laughed and stepped down and came over to the fire. "Why don't you tie your horse on back and ride inside? You look like you've been rough string ridin' all night."

I nodded and he kicked out the fire while I tied the horse on behind the coach, then I pulled myself inside. A drummer snored away and another man looked at me with that expression that only a southern gentleman can have.

Charlie got in and nudged me into a seat and the southern man said, "Can't he ride on top?"

"You don't like it, you ride on top," Charlie Hatch said, casually.

"It's not my custom to—"

"And it ain't my custom to tell a man somethin' twice," Charlie Hatch said. "So shut up." He turned to me as the coach lurched into motion. "Got your wire. Just happened to be in town. Lucky. I caught the next stage. Figured it would be as quick. Especially since I know the habits of a certain party and figured it was likely that he'd do one better than lightnin' and strike twice. Go ahead and get some sleep if you want."

"I don't feel too bad now," I told him. "Got any idea what time it is?"

"Oh, somewhere around four in the mornin'. Why?"

"I just like to know how much sleep I've been missing," I said.

Unknown to me I'd made camp not five miles from a stage relay station; when we stopped I got down and stamped my feet and the southern gentleman glared at me and went on inside. At the horse trough I washed my face and hands; Charlie Hatch sat at the curbing and rolled a cigaret and then said, "Buster, we might as well understand each other. We're going to bring The Dingo Kid back one way or another. He went back on his word to Shaw Buckner and that just won't do, Buster." When I opened my mouth to speak, he held up his hand. "All right, who shot that guard? Dandy or Dingo?"

"I guess Dingo did."

"You guess?"

"All right, Dingo did then!" I blew out a long breath. "Can't Shaw Buckner—"

"No he can't and you know it," Charlie quickly put in. "Dingo was welcome to do as he pleased but Shaw made it plain to him that he'd better never step out of line in his bailiwick. Now how much more can you do for a man?"

"Yeah, but the reason Dingo and Dandy—"

"Now just how much difference does that really make? Buster, there is always a reason and at the time it always sounds pretty good." He shook his head and crushed out his smoke. "Shaw knows why I wanted to take him back. Dingo and I are friends, same as you are and maybe I can do it without shooting him."

"That's been worrying me some too."

"Let's get back on the stage," Charlie said, because the driver swaggered out and climbed aboard. The shotgun guard mounted up and the stage had started to roll when the southerner dashed out and barely made it. He smelled strongly of whiskey and he panted as he fell back into his seat.

"Miserable service," he said. "A man hardly has time to take a leak around here." He took a handkerchief from his hip pocket and wiped his face and I saw the pistol in his belt and knew that Charlie had seen it too.

It was getting light out, a grayness that was turning pink over the mountains. Neither Charlie nor I felt like talk so we pulled our hats down over our eyes and dozed.

The day turned off hot and we made four more stops before sundown.

While the horses were being changed Charlie and I ate inside the station then went outside to talk. He said, "We should be in Billings come dawn. I kind of look for The Dingo Kid to make a move if he's goin' to." He busied himself with a smoke then passed the tobacco to me. "Wonder what that fella inside the coach will do? Throw up his hands or draw?"

"Maybe one of us ought to ride up on top from now on."

"I was thinkin' that," Charlie admitted. "I'll take care of the drummer and our whiskey drinkin' friend." He grinned. "If I have to hit him he'll take it more kindly than if you did it."

"If a man can take a thing like that kindly."

"Keep your eye on the shotgun guard though. I'd hate to see him cut down on Dingo and blow him in half."

"You really think he'll try to stick up the stage alone?"

"It's been done," Charlie said. He nudged me and we saw the driver and shotgun guard coming out.

Charlie got inside and I climbed on top with the luggage and the driver looked questioningly at me. "Just thought I'd change for a spell," I said, smiling. "I can stretch out up here."

"It does get cramped inside," the driver admitted and yelled the six-up span into the harness.

We bumped along and night started to come, dropping grayness down over the mountains and making deep shadows over everything. The road pitched and turned and the driver handled the stage from long practice over this road; all of them made driving seem easy.

After dark Charlie stuck his head out and said, "How's it up there, Buster?"

"Nice."

He pulled back in and we went on a few miles, the stage finally slowing as it topped a long rise. When the driver reached the summit he stopped the stage to give the horses a breather and something made me reach back to my saddle and draw my rifle from the scabbard.

I had hardly pulled it clear when a man said, "All right, reach!"

The shotgun guard jumped and started to lift his sawed-off and all I could do was hit him with my rifle barrel and watch him collapse and roll down into the forward boot. Inside the coach there was a meaty sound and a soft curse as Charlie disarmed the southern gentleman and I yelled, "Dingo, you damned fool! It's me, Buster!"

A man from the other side of the coach said, "Who the hell's Buster?" and let go with a sixgun. The bullet plowed across the roof of the coach and I realized that that wasn't Dingo at all. They were bandits and they were holding up the stage and I'd already gone ahead and knocked out the shotgun guard.

The driver jumped down, and just in time because from the other side three men opened up with sixguns and the roof of that coach became a hot place to be.

Charlie was shooting from inside the coach and I went to the ground and rolled under the coach as a horseman dashed in close; I could just make him out, a looming shadow and I tipped up the muzzle of the rifle and knocked him out of the saddle.

There was a lot of yelling going on.

"Pete! Pete! Did you get the shotgun?"

"Overhere! Overhere! Watch the guy on the roof!"

"Sonofabitch! Get the horses before they bolt!"

The drummer was on the floor of the coach, bleating like a wounded sheep and Charlie Hatch opened the door and came out in a roll. I was crouched nearby and he grunted in surprise when he found me, then he ducked under the coach and came up on the other side.

One of the bandits was approaching the head of the team, riding right down the road and when he got close, Charlie shot him out of the saddle. The man fell and the horses shied and backed up and the front rim of the coach rolled over my boot heel.

And that bandit was still yelling: "Pete! Pete! Dammit, Pete, get those horses! The rest of you keep your hands up!"

I don't know what he was thinking because we'd already shot two of them and to a man with a lick of sense that is not exactly the way things happen when everyone has their hands up.

Charlie was motioning for me to fall back and try and circle around and I crawled out under the rear axle and stood up. I could hear the other two bandits in the brush alongside the road; they should never have bunched up like that, both on each side and even I knew it and I had no experience at all as a stage bandit.

While I stood at the rear of the coach, Charlie Hatch crawled forward until he was by the off wheel and he reached inside the boot, fumbled around and found the guard's shotgun. Then he pointed it into the brush and rapidly fired both barrels, not really intending to hit anything, but he sure scared the hell out of them for they both bolted clear, shooting and wheeling their horses.

Of course he ducked down and got out of there and they shot holes in the front boot and bounced whining bullets off the wheel rims and gave me a chance to duck into the brush.

"Get the express box! Get the express box!" one yelled.

"Get it yourself, dammit!" I could make him out, sitting his horse, a lumpy shadow hurriedly punching spent shells from his pistol and trying to reload while his horse faunched around in the pitch darkness.

I could have dropped him with one shot, but

instead I said, "Throw up your hands! You're covered!"

My voice, from the brush, really startled him and I heard Charlie crash through the brush on the other side of the road and I knew we had them boxed.

"Come on! Throw 'em up!" I yelled. "You're cut off now!"

I really believe the man in the road intended to surrender; he started to put up his hands, but the other one, near the brush and farther down, started blazing away at me with his sixgun. The muzzle flash was a series of orange roses; he shot too fast for real effect although the bullets did come close.

Charlie Hatch shot twice; he had a gun in each hand and the bandit peeled off his horse and hit heavily in the dusty road. Unfortunately I took my attention off the rider I was supposed to be covering and he suddenly bolted and took off down the road, riding flat against the horse's neck and I didn't even bother to take a shot at him.

The driver cautiously showed himself and then the southern gentleman got down from the coach and the shotgun guard moaned and held his head and swore in a steady, droning tone of voice.

"Get a lantern," Charlie Hatch said to the driver and a moment later a match flared and the chimney clanked down and Charlie took the lantern and walked around, looking at the bandits.

He turned them over with his foot and shined the light in their faces.

"Say, ain't he—" I shut my mouth and looked at Charlie, who nodded.

"Yeah, one of Boxley's riders. Must have been broke and lookin' for some ready cash before gettin' out." The shotgun guard came up, rubbing his head. "Here, hold this," Charlie said, handing him the lantern.

The shotgun guard took it, grumbling, then looked at me. "What's the idea of hittin' me anyway?"

"He didn't want you to get shot," Charlie said, matter-of-factly. "Bring the light over here."

"Say, I don't like to be ordered around," the guard said. " 'Specially by people I don't know."

"I'm a deppitysheriff and so's he," Charlie said, jerking his thumb in my direction.

He could lie so sincerely that no one ever thought to disagree with him. The stage driver, who knew him, opened his mouth to say something then thought better of it and shook his head, remaining silent.

Charlie had the driver catch up the bandits' horses and tie them on behind and he made the southern gentleman help him load the dead men on top; he spared the shotgun guard the effort because he had a throbbing head.

Then he gave the driver back the lantern and winked at me. "You ride on top with the driver, deppity. And I'll put in my report that you done a good job tonight."

"Now you're just too blamed kind," I said, and climbed up beside the driver.

He nervously yelled the team into motion, then looked at me. "What the hell you and Charlie up to? How come you hit old Gabe on the head?"

"It looked to me like he was going to get shot," I said.

The driver laughed. "All right, so you won't tell me. But you kind of figured there'd be a holdup, huh?"

"That's a foolish notion if I ever heard one."

"You and him was mighty set for it."

"Just our cautious nature," I told him. "Looks to me like these were the same bunch that hit you before, huh?"

He shook his head. "Only two of 'em then."

"How do you know? The other two could have been in the brush."

"Then how come they didn't cut loose like they did tonight?" He peered at me through the darkness. "What you tryin' to say anyhow?"

"That they're the same bunch. What difference does it make? They didn't get anything either time."

"The luck's on my side," the driver said and kicked the metal express box. "Got nearly fifteen thousand in gold in it tonight. That's worth doin' a little shootin' over, ain't it?" He laughed and nudged me with his elbow. "Oh, that Charlie he plays a game close to his chest, don't he? Deppitysheriff, hahahahahahaha. He ain't never been a deppity nothin'."

"But you wouldn't go and spoil his fun, would you? After all, he went and hit that passenger and if it got out that Charlie wasn't the law, then he might complain to the line. Right?"

"Yeah, never thought of that."

At the next stage stop the agent got all excited when he found that we'd been held up and he got the hostlers to take the dead men down off the coach and taken around to the tack shed. The shotgun guard had to be helped inside; I'd hit him a lot harder than I thought and his scalp had been cut open and he was sick at his stomach. The southern gentleman was telling everyone what happened as though he had done it all by himself and the drygoods drummer headed for the bar and drank two shots of whiskey in a row before he became calm.

Charlie and I sat down to supper; it was stew and not bad either. We took our coffee outside and sat on the well curbing and finally he said, "You added up how many mistakes we made tonight and got away with?"

"No and I don't want to."

"Surprise you a little when you yelled and got shot at?"

"Almost wet my pants," I admitted. "I didn't figure on four of 'em. Did you?"

He laughed uneasily. "For a minute or two there I couldn't recollect when I'd been in anything any tighter than that."

"Yeah, Charlie, and if they'd known what they were doing we'd likely be dead."

"Now ain't that a cheerful thought."

13

OUR ARRIVAL in Billings set up quite a stir and the sheriff of Yellowstone County was particularly interested. The shotgun guard had already forgiven me the knot on the head and was convinced that only quick thinking on my part had saved his life. And the driver, who had spent the entire time crouched on the boot out of harm's way declared that our resistance was most heroic.

Even the southern gentleman, who emerged without a scratch, grudgingly declared that if Charlie Hatch hadn't belted him on the jaw and taken his pistol away from him he would probably have exposed himself and got killed because he was not a very good shot to begin with and for a moment there had allowed his bravery to override his good sense.

Through all this glowing testimony, including the drummer's statement, Charlie Hatch sat with a wide grin on his face and kept making depreciating remarks and gestures that meant, t'warn't nothin' at all.

I didn't say anything because no one asked me anything, and the way things were shaping up, talk would do more harm than good. The sheriff was a thorough, plodding man and by the time he had shooed the others out of his small office he had become pretty well convinced that these dead bandits were the same ones who had held up the stage before.

He offered Charlie and I cigars and smiled at us like a father who was very proud of his sons and took all the credit for it. But he was not a fool and he looked at me for a moment, then said, "What was that you yelled just before you hit the shotgun guard?"

"Why—ah—I don't remember," I said. "The first thing that came into my mind, I guess. Just trying to distract the bandits."

"That was quick thinkin' there, Buster," Charlie said, and I wondered what he really meant, what I'd said I'd done or what I'd just now told the sheriff.

"You saw the bandit before the shotgun guard did, huh?"

"That's about it. His head was turned the other way and I knew he'd be drilled before he could turn around. And I was sure the bandit hadn't seen me at all."

"It's likely you saved his life then," the sheriff said, and brushed his dense mustache. He looked at Charlie Hatch. "How come you went into action so fast?"

"I'm just naturally speedy. And I was lookin' out the window to see why we'd stopped and saw the bandit alongside the road." He grinned and tilted his cigar upward. "All along I'd figured that the gentleman ridin' across me was a natural-born hero and sure enough he pulled his pistol before he even knew what to shoot at. A thing like that can be dangerous, go off and hurt somebody, so I fetched him a lick in the chops."

The sheriff nodded and thought about it before speaking. "I'm a little bothered by this because I investigated the other holdup and clearly found the tracks of two riders. And only two. This time there were four. Don't seem to me to be the work of the same bunch."

"Likely it was the same two all right," Charlie said, easily. "It looks to me like they figured they'd do better with four men and talked a couple of down-and-outers to throw in with them." He shrugged. "But with three dead and the other lit out, it's hard to say which was the original two. Don't you agree?"

"That does make sense," the sheriff said. He looked from one to the other. "Didn't I hear some talk about you two being deputies?"

Charlie laughed and waved it all aside. "Oh, you know how it is, sheriff, everyone so blamed excited and all. I just told them that to calm 'em down. You know how it soothes folks to know that the law is handlin' everything."

"Well, it looks like you've done a good job for the county. You can go any time you feel like it. I don't have anything more to talk about."

"You could do us a little favor if you was so inclined," Charlie Hatch said.

"Such as?"

He put on a good show of embarrassment. "Buster and I had a little fallin' out with the sheriff at Miles City and I wondered if maybe you couldn't sort of make up some kind of a report for us to take back and let him know that we're not as bad as we sometimes behave."

He gave us that gimlet-eyed stare lawmen use when they suspect the worst. "Say, you two aren't wanted, are you?"

"Oh, no," Charlie said, quickly, too quickly I thought.

The sheriff thought so too because he said, "You two stick around town while I send a telegram. Don't try to leave because my deputies will be watching you. Now get out of here."

As soon as we got outside I said, "What the devil did you tell him a thing like that for?"

"I just couldn't ask him for an affidavit, could I?" He took my arm and steered me into the first saloon we came to and after we'd bought beers and found a table he let me in on the rest of it. "Now neither of us want Shaw Buckner to throw Dingo in jail. Right?"

"Right."

"But how're we goin' to do that if Dingo held up the stage?" I opened my mouth to tell him how and he shook his head, holding me silent. "The sheriff here will wire Buckner and ask if we're wanted. And Shaw will wire back and tell him no, but he'll be curious and want to know what's going on. So the sheriff here will tell him about how we shot up the bandits and Shaw will wire back and want to know all about that and—"

I started nodding and smiling. "—and pretty soon Shaw is going to find out that these bandits were the same ones who tried before and that'll mean that Dingo and Dandy didn't—"

"You're catchin' on right away there, Buster."

"Man, that's low down and sneaky."

"It is for a fact," Charlie Hatch admitted. "But since Dingo and Dandy didn't get a dime out of the holdup, I figure they rate one more chance. Knowin' that Shaw can't go back on his word, even if he wanted to, I figure it's up to us to clean this up. Right?"

"It's a pity you're not governor of the territory," I said.

He grinned. "I've always felt I was working way beneath my station in life. Finish your beer and let's find The Dingo Kid before he does somethin' stupid."

We tried a few places, figuring to run into him, then Charlie turned to the hotel and went up to

214

speak to the desk clerk. "Tell me, do you have a Mr. and Mrs. Nolan stayin' here?"

"Yes indeed. Room 26 at the end of the hallway."

Charlie nodded his thanks and went up. The hotel was an improvement over the one in Miles City, carpets in the hall and bright wallpaper on the walls. We found the room right off and Charlie knocked. Mrs. Nolan opened the door and stared at us a moment before she recognized us under our whiskers.

"Why, Mr. Hatch, do come in!"

She was heavy with child and it taxed her to move around; we stepped inside and stood there, indicating that we couldn't stay.

"Is Sad-eye here?" Charlie asked.

"No, he's working. Got a job right off at the lumber yard. You'll find him there."

"Thank you," Charlie said. "I hope you're feelin' well, Mrs. Nolan."

"It's not a poorly feeling I mind," she said. "There's nothing wrong, is there?"

"No," Charlie said. "We were just lookin' for The Dingo Kid, that's all."

She seemed very surprised. "Why, he's working at the lumber yard with my husband."

"Wouldn't you know it," Charlie said. "Thanks. We may see you again before we leave town."

We backed out, smiling and nodding, then hurried on down the stairs and paused in the lobby only long enough to ask directions to the lumber yard. It was on the south edge of town and we found the foreman in his small office.

"You got two men working here called Dingo and Sad-eye?"

"Yup. You'll find 'em across the yard loadin' mining stumping."

They were there all right, loading onto wagons and neither saw us as we came up. Charlie said, "Dingo, I ought to kick your stupid head in."

He almost dropped the end he was lifting; they threw it on the wagon and The Dingo Kid turned to face us. He grinned hugely, then let it fade.

"Now, Charlie, don't be a sorehead."

"I ought to fire your ass right here and now!" He looked at Sad-eye Nolan. "I suppose you two talked it over and decided it was better for him to stay here than to go back."

"It did come up in the conversation," Sad-eye admitted.

"Well, Dingo's goin' back," Charlie said. "I've gone to too much trouble fixin' it up so you won't have to go to jail. But right now I'm not sure I did right." He jerked his thumb toward the foreman's shack across the yard. "Go draw your time. We'll leave on the eastbound stage."

"How's Dandy?" Dingo asked.

"He's back at Moon Creek by now," Charlie told him.

"I would never have left him if the girl hadn't been takin' care of him." He took off his gloves and put them in his belt. "Charlie, I made a lot of mistakes, huh?"

"One after another. And when you get back you're going to get every dirty cowboyin' job I can hunt up for you. You're goin' to winter out in the lonesomest place I can find and come spring roundup you're going to eat dust and ride bog and hay and fix fence and shovel manure. And if I ever think you're even thinkin' about easy money I'll stomp a mudhole in your head."

"You sure you got this squared with Shaw Buckner? I gave him my word and—"

"And you broke it," Charlie said flatly. "Go get your time, Dingo. We'll wait here."

He shrugged and walked off and Sad-eye watched him go. "He's been doin' a lot of lookin' over his shoulder lately, Charlie. Damned fool. We bumped into each other accidentally. He was lookin' in a store window and I happened to be walkin' to the hotel from work and seen him." Then he grinned. "Sure nice to see you fellas. Be nice to get back to my regular work."

"You just take care of your wife," Charlie told him. "And try and get back before the roads close. I've got two men on your job now and it's more than they can handle and the brand can't afford that kind of money when we can get a dumbbell like you to do it." He reached out and snapped Sad-eye's hat down over his eyes. "Take care of yourself."

We went back to the foreman's shack where Dingo was getting paid off. He looked at Charlie Hatch and said, "Knew I was goin' to lose somethin' the minute I laid eyes on you."

"He'd quit sooner or later anyway," Charlie said. "Come on, Dingo. Where's your gear?"

"A rooming house near the edge of town."

We went there and got it and Charlie acted as though he didn't dare let Dingo out of his sight and that smarted but he was rubbing it in and Dingo was taking it because he knew he had it coming, and a lot worse.

That evening we had our supper in the hotel and while we were eating Charlie Hatch nudged me and I looked around in time to see Nan Wilson come in with a splendidly dressed man. He saw that she was seated and snapped his fingers to get the waiter's attention. While he was ordering, Nan looked around and saw me sitting there and her complexion turned chalky and she raised a hand quickly to her breast as though she were suddenly short of breath.

She spoke earnestly to the man and he got up and left the dining room, on some errand for her. Then she got up and came over to our table.

She spoke to me. "I suppose you're going to spoil this for me. Revenge, isn't it?"

"You got another man to keep you," I said, gently. "No, I'm not going to spoil it. How could I? You might as well play out the game as long as your looks hold out. You're near thirty. Next year it'll be another man, not as wealthy or as fine as this, and each time the man will be less because you'll have less to offer. And you think I'll spoil it?" I shook my head. "Go back to your table and your life and leave me alone."

She acted as though she intended to speak but somehow I'd said it all for her; she turned and went back and was sitting there patiently when her man came back and she gave him a huge, dazzling smile.

The Dingo Kid had observed all this carefully. He said, "Is there anything about this I ought to know?"

"It's Buster's business," Charlie said. "Leave it that way."

"All right by me," Dingo said, and felt a little shut out.

"She's the woman I'm supposed to have molested in Texas," I said.

He turned and looked at her. "Hell, I wouldn't mind molesting her myself."

"Wait another five years," Charlie said, "and you can have her."

"In five years I wouldn't want her," Dingo said, not really knowing that he was pronouncing sentence on Nan Wilson.

The waiter brought the meal, three huge platters, and Charlie said, "This is on you, Dingo. I'm going to let you get the stage fares too."

"For Christ sake, you're going to take all I earned!"

"You're gettin' off damned cheap," Charlie Hatch said. "And you know it." Then he grinned. "Dingo, are you really worth all this trouble? Do you realize I'll have to explain like hell to O. B. when I get back? And Bullmoose Reilly is going to roar like a stuck heifer. And Shaw's no fool. He'll never really be convinced that you and Dandy didn't try to roadagent that stage."

"My mother always said I was a problem."

"Your mother was right," Charlie said.

When it came stage time, we waited on the porch and then the sheriff came down the street just as we were going to get on. "Hold up there," the sheriff said and put his hand on the coach door. "You're Charlie Hatch, foreman at Broken T." He speared Dingo with his finger. "And you're The Dingo Kid, the famous outlaw."

"Aw, I ain't really famous," Dingo said. "It's mostly lies."

"You're a roadagent and I found a dodger on you from Arizona."

"I've given all that up," Dingo said. "Been goin' straight and sendin' money home regular to my mother and crippled sister."

The sheriff stared at Dingo for a moment, then looked at Charlie Hatch. "Is he lyin' to me? Aw, never mind. Get the hell out of my county, the three of you."

"You're a man with a soul," Charlie said, and urged us on the stage. There was one other passenger, an elderly woman so I gave her my seat and climbed up on top.

The driver was the same one who had driven the westbound and he said, "Let's have a nice quiet trip, shall we?"

"Suits me."

I don't think he believed it.

The trip back was no different from the trip out, except that we didn't get held up and we were going back and I realized that the destination of a stage really didn't mean much to the driver; it was only important to the passenger, who had a job waiting, or a wife or trouble, or just something different.

Charlie Hatch entertained the lady passenger with stirring accounts of his life and I could hear her laugh now and then. At the first stage stop we picked up another passenger and The Dingo Kid joined me atop the coach.

He stretched out and braced his feet against the luggage rails to keep from getting pitched off. "That girl take pretty good care of Dandy, Buster?"

"Better than you think."

"I guess she turned out prettier than he first thought." He looked at me.

"They all do, Dingo. They all do."

"Are you goin' back to Texas now?"

It was a question I hadn't really asked myself, but it was time for an answer and I had no trouble deciding. "No. I'll get my wife to sell my place and we'll find something here."

"You going to stay on at Broken T?"

I shook my head. "A place of my own, maybe. A man wants to be with his family. I married a woman, Dingo, not a brand."

Then The Dingo Kid hooked his hands around the luggage railing and hung head down so that he could look inside the coach. "Hey, Charlie, Buster's going to send for his wife and kids and quit cowboyin'."

"Hell, I know that," Charlie said. "You're dumb, Dingo." He cranked himself half out of the window and looked over the top, his grin splitting his face from ear to ear. "I figure on gettin' Shaw Buckner to give him a job as deputy sheriff. The pay's good and he'll be home most nights."

"Bet you don't swing that," Dingo said.

"How much?"

"Twenty dollars."

"You're on," Charlie said and they shook hands, which just about cost both of them their balance.

The driver looked around, his expression a bit dour. "You two fellas mind makin' up your minds whether you want to ride inside or out?" Charlie drew back inside and The Dingo Kid rolled over on his stomach and hooked his bootheels into the railing and watched the road winding away behind. The driver looked at me and grinned. "That Charlie, he's a real son of a gun. He'll do it too!"

"Looks like," I said, and decided that this living was really something and certainly worth all the trouble a man had to put up with sometimes just to go on with it.

Center Point Publishing

600 Brooks Road • PO Box 1
Thorndike ME 04986-0001 USA

(207) 568-3717

**US & Canada:
1 800 929-9108**
www.centerpointlargeprint.com